THE SEVEN STONES

THE SEVEN STONES

KIMBERLY ASHLEY

Anamcara Press LLC

Published in 2024 by Anamcara Press LLC
Author © 2024 by Kimberly Ashley
Cover & Book design by Maureen Carroll
Adobe Caslon Pro, Tsisquilisda, Berlin Sans FB
Printed in the United States of America.

Book Description: In a world shattered by darkness, Kadya and Ruark embark on a perilous journey to find their missing family. Guided by the brilliance of a mysterious gem, they navigate treacherous landscapes, encounter unexpected allies, and face their deepest fears. As they draw closer to the truth, they must unravel the ancient secrets hidden within the stones, for their destiny and the fate of their loved ones depend on it.

ANAMCARA PRESS LLC
P.O. Box 442072, Lawrence, KS 66044
https://anamcara-press.com/

Ordering Information:
Quantity sales. Special discounts are available on quantity purchases by corporations, associations, and others. For details, contact the publisher at the address above.
Orders by U.S. trade bookstores and wholesalers. Please contact Ingram Distribution.
The Seven Stones; ISBN-13: 978-1-960462-10-7 eBook
The Seven Stones; ISBN-13: 978-1-960462-09-1 paperback

YAF001020 YOUNG ADULT FICTION / Action & Adventure / Survival Stories
YAF024110 YOUNG ADULT FICTION / Historical / Prehistory
YAF066000 YOUNG ADULT FICTION / Visionary & Metaphysical
YAF038000 YOUNG ADULT FICTION / Magical Realism

Library of Congress Control Number: 2023939356

For my students

Chapter 1

The gem glistened in the dazzling sunlight. They could see it from the precipice where they stood. It was brilliant against the rocky canyon wall, and beckoned to them with a soft, pink glow.

Mesmerized, Ruark and Kadya took in the rare beauty.

"Is it the pink stone?" Kadya asked

Ruark watched the shimmering light. "What else could it be? We have to get closer to find out."

They looked to the left and the right.

"Careful, Kadya!" Ruark warned.

Her feet were perilously close to the edge as she peered down at the meandering river far below.

"I do not see a way to the other side," she said, stepping back. "Is there an easier crossing?"

She watched her brother survey their surroundings, taking in the vast distance while considering how far they had come.

"It might take days to find a path." He moved between her and the dangerous edge of the cliff. "We should move to lower ground and settle in before nightfall. The fastest way will be along the river."

Kadya followed Ruark behind a massive rock, going down toward more level ground where they would eventually reach the river's edge.

"We need to get set up camp before sundown," he reminded.

Her feet were sore from endless days of walking. Today was the seventh day since the attack on their village and the seventh day of not knowing what had happened to their parents and younger sister, Tawnee.

They had slept in caves, weathered rain, and wandered through the dense forest hoping to find someone from their village. They dared not go too close, afraid of what they might find. They hunted small game and fished in the river, always on the lookout for wild berries and pine nuts.

"Ruark, can we stop?" she asked, sitting before he answered.

Silhouetted against a huge rock, she rubbed the dirt from her ankle, avoiding the blister on the back of her heel. She pulled the small hair rod from her hair. It had been carved by her grandfather with a face of a child surrounded by leaves and vines. Her mother had given it to her recently, reminding her it was only a matter of time before she was to have a family of her own. She placed it into the fold of her waist pocket and massaged her head.

She did not want a family of her own. She envied her brother's freedom and enjoyed hunting more than the mundane tasks left to women of their village. In fact, she and Ruark had been checking some traps for their father on the day they noticed plumes of smoke rising from the valley and heard the chilling screams. They had no choice but to flee.

"Do you think we can ever go back to the village?" she asked.

Ruark leaned against a tree. He wound a piece of hide between his fingers. "I think about it all the time."

Ruark was tall and lean. His dark hair accentuated his eyes. He looked older than his sixteen years.

"There may be nothing left," he added.

She cut him off. She did not want to remember that terrible day.

"I know we could not have gone back then, but it has been seven nights. We have not seen or heard anyone." She hesitated, thinking of her mother and father, "What if they are looking for us?"

"If they are looking for us, they will find us," he said, looking away.

Kadya sighed. It was so like him to avoid the obvious question. What if they were not looking for them because they could not?

She knew there was no use arguing when he had his mind set. "I just want to find them."

"As do I," Ruark said quietly. "I have to believe we will."

He looked across the canyon at the pink light embedded in the mountainside. He reached into his pack and took out the blue stone they had found several nights earlier.

"Kadya, all this time the stones have not shown their lights. They have been hidden and only talked about in stories. Why now?"

"I do not know," she said, captivated by the blue glow. She remembered the night they found it, two nights after the attack. They had fallen asleep in a small cave, weary and exhausted. Only a few embers remained where a fire had blazed earlier outside the cave. Kadya woke to a shimmering blue light on the cavern wall. Rubbing her eyes in disbelief, she stood and stumbled towards it. The brilliant sheen came from a small ledge, too high for her to reach. The closer she went, the brighter it gleamed.

"Ruark, look!"

He stirred but did not answer.

"Ruark, wake up! You must see this!"

"Where are you?" he answered groggily.

"I am here. What is that?"

He rose to move toward Kadya's outline in the bluish light and reached overhead. He seized upon a small glowing rock. She followed him to where they had been sleeping. They sat in silence, astonished at the sight.

When Ruark finally spoke, his words were slow and deliberate. "I think it might be one of the seven stones."

"The seven stones?" Kadya answered.

"The seven stones of our ancestors. The Old Ones speak of them in their stories."

"Yes, I remember. But I did not think the stories were real!"

Ruark remained intent, his eyes on the stone. "It is said they can only be seen by those who have pure hearts. Others see only regular stones. They cannot receive their power."

Several moments passed before he continued. "They say children always see them."

They stared into the blue stillness that seemed to grow brighter.

Ruark's voice grew solemn, "Our people, the people of the Yolan were guardians of the stones until they were taken by the Malevo many years ago."

"The Malevo?"

"According to the stories, they were ancient cousins

of our people, always wanting war. They scoffed at the prosperity of our ancestors. Father told me they lived in fear and want."

"Why?" Kadya asked. She wanted to understand all she could about the shimmering blue stone that lit the entire cave like daylight.

"They looked like regular stones to the Malevo. They could not see their worth or benefit from their power."

"Is that why they took them?"

"I suppose. The Malevo were envious and wanted them for themselves, even though they could never see their glow."

"Maybe they did not want anyone else to have them," Kadya added.

"Possibly," Ruark shrugged.

The quietness of the cave enveloped them. The eerie beauty of the stone's blue sheen reflected from their faces.

"Father has told you so much about the stones. Tell me more."

Ruark gathered his thoughts before speaking.

"There are seven altogether. Each one offers a particular value for those who are worthy. They are most powerful when they are all together."

His voice broke. Kadya knew he was thinking about the attack on their village. The thought made her eyes well with tears.

"This stone brought peace to our people and protected them from enemies. According to the stories, our people have felt threatened ever since. Before that time, we lived in peace with our neighbors. No one dared to attack us."

Ruark got up to stoke the fire. When he returned, Kadya was full of questions.

"Do you remember what the other stones bring?"

"It has been so long since Father and I spoke of it. There is a stone of wisdom. It is black with a deep purple glow. The red stone offers courage. The clear white stone of harmony was broken and scattered."

"Is that the one mother sings about—with glittering stones that shine like stars?"

Ruark nodded and counted on his fingers to recall the other stones.

"The orange stone is for healing and one of them offers abundance. I think it is yellow."

He thought for a moment. "I cannot remember what the pink stone offers."

"Are they all this size?" she asked in wonder at the stone not even the size of her fist. How could such small objects have so much power and cause so much trouble?

"I cannot believe we found one here, tonight, in this cave," Ruark said.

Kadya could hear the excitement rising in his voice. He picked up the stone and held it, memorizing every detail.

"The stone may have led us here," he said abruptly.

Kadya watched the blue stone, now brilliant in the small cave. Glints of bright blue reflected in her eyes.

Ruark placed the stone down and shifted to lie on his side. "We can search for the other stones," he said earnestly. "If this stone led us here, I believe it will lead us to the others in time. It may be our only hope."

Kadya frowned. What did he mean by 'their only hope'?

"How," she asked. "We have no way of knowing where the others might be. They were lost so long ago.

Where would we start?" To think the stones were reaching out to them was too much for her to imagine. Could the stones really be calling to them?

"We can start right here in this cave," Ruark said, pulling her from her spiraling thoughts. He settled his head on his arm, turning away from her. "Tomorrow will be a long day. Try to get some sleep."

Kadya stared into the blue light, alone with her thoughts, haunted by the familiar fear to which she had grown accustomed.

✳✳✳

Since that night in the cave, searching for the stones had formed their days, giving them purpose beyond the aimless wandering and painful loss. Most nights, they fell asleep under an endless sky, lit with a million stars.

Today, across the vast divide, they could see the sparkling pink glow, high on the steep incline. Ruark walked to the clearing and looked across the valley.

"The pink stone offers empathy. Tomorrow, we will go."

Chapter 2

Ruark and Kadya could see the pink stone shimmering. It drew them towards it. Sometimes it was out of view as they rounded a bend or walked through a patch of forest. By mid-afternoon, it was still so far away. They stopped to fish in a small lake.

"When we get there, we will have to climb that cliff. It might not be possible," Ruark said.

"How many days do you think it will take?"

"Two, maybe three."

Ruark pointed at a trout swimming near the surface of the water. He had been trying to teach her to catch a fish with her hands. She spent most of her time gathering food and tending the plants and herbs that grew near the village. Although she was quite skilled with a bow and much preferred hunting, fishing was proving to be more difficult.

After several attempts, she threw herself down in the sand. She had other things on her mind.

Ruark laughed at her and kept fishing.

"I know empathy is being able to see from someone's point of view and feel what they feel. But how can a stone do that?"

"The stones do not do anything. The empathy is offered and must be received."

"So, the stones remind people what they should do?"

"Perhaps. Father told me stories about the stones, but I thought they were made up and exaggerated by the old ones to entertain us. I never ask how they worked."

Suddenly, Ruark grabbed a fish and heaved it onto the sand. He walked out of the water to gather his catch and prepare a fire. He took out his fire sticks and began to rub them together.

Kadya admired how easily he did everything. He had learned well from their father to survive away from the village.

"I am not that fast at making a fire," she admitted aloud.

Ruark remained intent on his work. He asked, "Do you remember when I spent eight days alone on the mountain for my initiation?"

"Yes, I remember."

He laughed, "Well, I spent the first couple of days trying to make a fire. When I finally had it figured out," he paused and grinned, "I was no longer cold."

Kadya chuckled at his admission of freezing to death on the mountain. "I am glad I did not have to do that."

He went back to his task. He fidgeted with a piece of hide, waiting for the fire to burn down. It was good to hear him laugh. He had barely spoken in the hours they walked. Now he looked across the valley to see if the stone was still visible. Kadya could see the concern on his face.

"You seem troubled," she said softly.

He placed the trout on the sticks and held them over the fire.

"I keep thinking about what happened that day in our village and how alone we are if we cannot find our parents and Tawnee. I worry about what we will do."

"We will find them!" Kadya said with a rush of determination to shake her alarm. She moved closer to the fire. The scent of the cooking trout gave her a sense of calm. "You worry about me too much."

"I know you are strong," he said, looking down at the sand.

His dark eyes reflected the light of the fire. "Honestly, it frightens me to go back to the village. But I think we should. We need to know what happened. Perhaps our parents and sister are there."

Kadya was stunned by his confession. She was not used to hearing him talk like this.

"Besides," he continued. "I do not think we can reach that stone easily. It is steep and rocky terrain."

Kadya shrugged. She waited for him to continue. He looked at the river, avoiding her gaze. She could not shake the desperate hope and fear of discovering if their village had survived the raid or if their parents were alive. Secretly, she hoped he wanted to stop chasing the pink stone and return to the village.

"What about the pink stone?" she asked.

"It will have to wait. The stones watched over our people. They will watch over us. We will change directions and head upriver toward the village. It will take many days."

He took the trout off the stick and placed it next to her. He motioned for her to eat. They shared it, even though it was not enough for the two of them.

"We have the blue stone," he said finally, checking the pack he always wore around his waist. It was secure. Kadya watched him squeeze his hand around it.

"We should go now. We need to make it to the valley by evening."

When they reached the river, the fast-moving water was so loud they could not hear each other speak. Overhead, the trees were thick, with little view of the open sky. The cool air was heavy with the scent of pine and spruce. When the valley widened again, they came to a meadow. The river was calm and looked like a deep pool. The sun had dipped below the horizon. They would need to find shelter for the night.

Ruark noticed evidence of a recently burned fire. A little farther away was another circle of charred wood, indicating a second fire. He crouched to examine the area.

"These fire rings are recent."

Kadya joined him, the hair standing on the back of her neck. Someone could be watching them. Until now, they had seen no one since the attack.

"A small group of ten or more travelers have been here, perhaps this morning."

She waited for him to speak while he studied the tracks.

"They are going upriver," he said, pointing his finger.

Hope surged through her. "They might be survivors from our village," she exclaimed, "our parents?"

The scent of the burned-out fires lingered in the cool evening air.

Ruark grew cautious, "We should move higher into the trees to find shelter for the night. We must stay hidden until we know who they are."

Thoughts of her parents and her sister flooded through her mind. It was almost dark. The azure sky was pierced by stars. A light chill and the heavy scent of pine made her sleepy. She longed to be in the comfort of her parents' home in the village, but she quickly pushed the thought aside.

"Ruark, I think this is a good place to stop." She motioned toward a grove of trees. Their dark shadows loomed against the evening sky.

He followed her and began ripping branches from the nearby evergreen bushes to form a shelter around the bottom of a tree trunk.

"We will have to do without a fire tonight. All we have are a few berries left from earlier today. I will get us a proper meal in the morning, but it is best if we get some rest. We can get an early start tomorrow."

Kadya did not question his decision. She secured the branches for their shelter and turned away his offer of a few berries. It would only make her hungrier. Drinking water from the stream would be enough.

Thoughts of their life before the raid and the faces of her family were all she could think about as they lay back-to-back for warmth, tired and hungry, before she fell asleep.

Chapter 3

A crescent moon gleamed high in the sky. Ruark was startled awake. He strained to see through the shadows. Careful not to move or make a sound, he remained calm. The white stripe of a skunk passed by on the other side of the tree branches and walked up the hill.

He was wide awake now and unsure how long until daylight. With so much to think about, it was impossible to lie still. The dim light was just enough to see a path to the river.

Leaving Kadya, he made his way to the riverbank. He sat and listened to the sound of the water. It rippled gently against the rocks. His growling stomach reminded him they would need to keep stocked with food.

He thought about the day to come and his concerns. Who had made the fire rings? Should they try to find out?

He dozed off by the river until sunlight streaked across the morning sky, then got out his fishing supplies. They had gone to sleep hungry. He did not want to run out of food again.

Kadya was greeted by the crackle of the fire and the

scent of cooking trout when she woke.

"I did not move once last night," she said, rubbing her back.

Ruark cooked the rest of the meat and wrapped it in leaves to store in his pack.

"Eat," he said, "it will be a long day. Watch for any game. We can stop to hunt along the way."

His words made her smile. Using a bow was her favorite thing to do.

They ate in silence and doused the fire. After gathering their few possessions, they continued along the river until it turned to rapids, then they moved to higher ground.

Climbing through the trees, they rounded a curve and heard the roar of water falling into a pool. Amazed by the sound, they drew closer to absorb the breath-taking sight. Water fell from high above them. Curious, Ruark took the lead. Kadya followed him over logs and boulders until they were near the top.

They stepped onto a ledge that made it possible to cross behind the falling water. The cool mist sprayed their faces. They walked with their backs to the wall. The noise made it impossible to speak.

Abruptly, Kadya stopped. She put a hand over her mouth. Ruark turned to see where she was looking. A glimmer of yellow emanated from the rock wall behind them.

The shimmering yellow light had to be another stone.

They edged near the stone. Ruark pried it loose from its resting place. Kadya leaned closer to see the stone's lustrous color. He grasped it tightly as they walked to the other side.

"Ruark, you said the stones would lead us. What can this mean?"

He did not respond. They climbed off the ledge onto a pile of boulders at the forest's edge. He knelt and took out the blue stone. He placed them together.

Kadya joined him. "They are beautiful," she gasped.

"The blue stone of peace and the yellow stone of abundance," he said under his breath. "Thinking about what is good and looking for the good in things makes more good things happen, creating abundance.

"Abundance," Kadya repeated. "Mother uses that word all the time. It means plenty. She tells us to keep gathering so we will have an abundance."

He watched her melancholy return. He knew she missed their mother. He did, too. He tried to cheer her up. "The stories of our ancestors are happy stories. They worked together and believed there would be enough for everyone, and it came to be."

"But the stones were taken!" she retorted.

"True," said Ruark. "Father warned me. He told me not all our people could see the stones. Some chose to be prideful and selfish."

"Is that why they were taken?" She watched him put the stones in his pack.

He was about to answer when he stopped, signaling her to stay quiet.

He took his bow and handed it to her. He gave her an arrow. She saw the rabbit in the undergrowth and quickly let the arrow fly. It struck below the neck.

"Nice, work!" Ruark cheered. He retrieved his arrow and threw the dead creature over his shoulder. He would skin and clean it later. They would have plenty of food for the next day.

The pair continued across the mountainside, creating a path as they went. By late afternoon, they made their way to the valley, closer to the river.

Ruark grew cautious. "Look how the grass lays over. There are footprints in the mud. Possibly ten or fifteen people are up ahead."

"Did they make the fire rings?" she asked.

"Maybe, but there could be others in the area."

"If only we knew who they were," she moaned. "Can we follow them?"

Ruark did not answer. He was alert to the possibility of danger. "We should stop here and cook the meat while it is daylight. We may be able to get closer, but we will have to be careful."

"I want to follow them," she persisted. "We must find out who they are."

"We can follow them, but we must keep a safe distance until we know."

Kadya started the fire this time. Then she leaned against the trunk of the tree. She stared at the clouds moving in large white puffs.

Before long, the scent of cooking meat filled the air.

"That smells so good!" she exclaimed.

While they ate, the unanswered question of who else was in the valley hung between them.

"We can travel for a while. It is still daylight. We should get going," Ruark said. He gathered his supplies. Kadya put out the fire, making sure there were no embers left.

They continued upriver along the water's edge. Lush vegetation grew thick and green, obscuring the view ahead.

"I smell smoke," Kadya said at once.

Ruark directed her into the trees. Perhaps they should have made camp earlier. They walked higher on the hillside through the undergrowth until they found a clearing.

"There they are," Kadya whispered.

Ruark saw the two fires near the river. He had to hold her back when she saw them.

"We must wait. We will know who they are soon enough," he whispered.

"It might be our parents looking for us," she said urgently.

"I hope it is," he said gently, feeling her relax at the thought.

"We will make camp here," Ruark said. "We have to keep a safe distance."

He planned to scout the situation after Kadya was asleep. He did not want to cause her to panic. He hoped to give her the news she craved.

As darkness fell across the valley, she finally closed her eyes from exhaustion.

Ruark went down the hillside. When he was close enough, he saw piles of supplies strewn around the campsite. Sitting around one of the fires were two men he did not recognize. They talked and smoked a pipe. He counted seven small forms lying on the ground around the other fire. They had to be children.

Kadya was sleeping when he returned. His mind was racing. It would be difficult to explain what he saw. It was odd to find children traveling with two men. It was not the way of his people.

He found a place to settle, careful not to wake her. Only then did notice his own disappointment. These strangers were not his parents. What had happened to them?

Lying back, he drifted into a restless sleep.

Chapter 4

Kadya was staring at him when he woke up. Gravely, she said, "I know you left last night. I heard you leave. What did you find?"

He rubbed his eyes and collected his thoughts. "I found them, but it was not anyone we know. I saw two men, not our parents."

Kadya's disappointment was palpable.

He waited a few moments before telling her the rest. "I think the others were children."

"Children?" Her voice trailed off.

"I know. It does not make sense. I saw two men sitting around one fire and seven children sleeping around the other fire."

She looked away helplessly. "I want to see Mother! I want her to say, 'Wake up, Kadya. It is all a bad dream.'"

"I know you do, but you must stay strong. Mother often talked about having strength for tough times. If she were here, what would she say to us?"

Kadya looked at the pebble-strewn pathway. She remembered her mother's face. "She would say this is one of those times!"

Ruark gathered his belongings. He slung his bow

over his back. "We should get moving. We can keep hidden and still make good time. I think it is best to avoid the men with the children and not get too close."

Kadya wiped her eyes and secured her few supplies into the pockets of her dress. She got up slowly but did not speak.

The strange party was gone when they got to the river. They had left behind no sign except the burnt-out fires.

After they walked for several hours, Ruark moved behind a large boulder and motioned for Kadya to do the same. Across the stream, they saw a boy walking on a fallen tree log. He was looking for something along the water's edge. He seemed very intent on his search. Suddenly, he jumped off and disappeared into the trees.

"Who was that?" Kadya asked.

"He looks too big to be one of the children I saw last night."

Ruark wanted to follow him, but he did not want to put Kadya in danger.

They walked across the meadow beside a rippling stream. Groves of poplar trees shimmied in the sunlight. Kadya turned to ask Ruark a question when the same boy jumped into the path in front of them.

"What are you doing?" he asked sharply. "Why do you follow us?"

He was not a boy but a young man about their age. He was not much taller than Kadya.

He continued, "I saw you this morning."

So, they were being watched. Ruark knew not to give anything away. The less he said, the more the stranger might reveal. His father had taught him that. He hoped Kadya would stay quiet.

"We are delivering a message to our village," Ruark said quickly.

"A message about what?" the young man asked pointedly. He wore skins like Ruark, with an open vest revealing his chest. His dark curly hair fell against his bare shoulders. It was held with a band tied around his head. His deep-set eyes taunted Ruark.

"There is no one in the village you seek. Everyone is gone."

Kadya moaned but remained steady. Ruark grew uneasy and stared at him without a response. He wanted to figure out what this stranger knew.

"I am Pak. My father is up ahead. He wants to know why you follow us."

Ruark wondered how long the men had known of their presence in the valley. "We are to bring a message to our village," he lied calmly. He tried not to betray his rising fear. "But if no one is there, then we will turn and go back."

Pak laughed. "I do not believe you."

Ruark's impatience with this stranger was growing. Kadya was staring at the ground. He wanted to ease her suffering.

He hoped Pak might reveal more about himself. Ruark asked, "What does it matter to you where we go?"

"It is nothing to me!" Pak sneered.

"Then let us be on our way," Ruark answered.

Pak squinted with a hateful look, "Do your people know of the seven stones?"

Ruark shifted, startled by the question. Could Pak see the stones? He tried desperately not to reach for his pack.

"What stones?" he lied.

"My people seek the stones. They were scattered," Pak proclaimed. His tone was arrogant.

Ruark wondered why he was talking of the stones.

It seemed foolish. He rested his hand against the two stones secure in his pack. "Why do your people seek them?" he goaded. He wanted Pak to reveal more.

Pak ignored the question. "They have searched for generations. I search with my father as my father searched with his father. We will search until we find them."

"How did they become scattered?" Ruark asked. He looked at Kadya. She stepped forward slightly, to listen to what Pak was going to say.

"There was a time when my people thought the stones would bring good fortune. They kept them in a sacred place."

"Where did they get them?" Ruark knew the answer from the stories his father told but he wanted to know what Pak knew.

Pak grew sullen and said, "What do you mean?"

"How were they lost?" Ruark asked.

"Someone tricked them," he said insolently.

Ruark could tell Pak was irritated, but he pressed him anyway. "How were they tricked?"

Pak seemed angry and refused to answer. Instead, he said, "I must go. It is better if you do not follow us. Go back from where you came."

Ruark was silent. He watched the young man turn and disappear into the forest.

Kadya asked, "Why is he so angry?"

"Because he doesn't know a better way," Ruark answered, remembering his father's words.

Ruark was upset by the strange interaction. "Kadya, they think we are following them. We must be going in the same direction."

"And they know what happened to our village," Kadya added dryly.

Ruark squatted on the ground to decide what to do. The sun was high in the sky. An eagle soared overhead in the stillness. They could bypass the group to get to the village or stay a comfortable distance behind them. They would find out soon enough what happened to the village.

"How does he know about the stones?" she asked.

Ruark answered solemnly, eyes fixed on the ground. "His people must be descendants of the Malevo. They lost the stones. They could not see their glow or receive their powers."

He stood and looked into the distance before continuing, "They lost hope. Their greed and desire were so great. They could not see what they had.

"I do not think he can see the stones," Kadya replied. "They are in your pack. I can see them."

"You are right. Pak cannot see the stones glow. He is full of anger and hate. He says they are searching for the stones as his father and grandfather searched. But they do not know what they are searching for because they cannot see their glow. They will never find them."

"Is it possible for them to ever see them?" Kadya asked.

"Father said it is difficult to see them again. A person must have a change of heart. Something inside must change to see the stones again. It is important to never lose sight of them in the first place."

He knew Kadya was thinking about his answer. There was so much to know about the history of their people and the stones. If talking about it helped to take her mind off of her sadness, he would tell her as much as he could remember. He still could not believe the stones were real.

"It seems like a never-ending problem if you cannot

see them glow. Why do our people not search for the stones?" she asked.

He did not know the answer. "That is a good question. Perhaps their faith in the stones' ability to know their hearts makes it possible..." He fumbled at the words.

"To receive their power?" Kadya finished his sentence.

"Yes, something like that. I don't know. Father and I never talked about it."

Kadya grew quiet. "Ruark, Pak said the people in our village are gone."

Ruark deflected, "The men know we are here. We should try to avoid them. They will be watching us."

Kadya was visibly shaken. He tried to set her mind at ease. "Soon we will be at the village. I think they will stop with the children well before dark. That will help us make up for lost time and go around them. It will be risky traveling at night."

"It is a risk I am willing to take," Kadya added firmly.

When the moon was overhead, they started up the mountain. They traveled high along the ridge, well within the trees. The tall pines soared above them on the dimly lit path. They made progress but needed to find a place to rest.

Through an opening in the trees, Ruark could see into the valley. He was disappointed to see the double fires.

"I hope we are a safe distance away. We can keep going or stop for the night," he said.

"I want to stop," Kadya said, frustrated by the sight. She began the nightly search for a place to sleep.

They sat to share the remains of their food rations for the day.

"When their fires are out, I am going down there."

'Can I go with you?" Kadya pleaded.

"No Kadya."

She would have no choice. He would wait until she was in a sound sleep.

***

He made no sound as he went down the mountain. When he reached the valley, he came out into the open, keeping low to the ground. He wanted to know more about the children. When he was close enough, a chill ran up his spine. He recognized their faces. Lying on the ground asleep was his sister, Tawnee.

Chapter 5

Ruark did not want to wake Kadya with the news. He needed time to think. Of course, they had to keep close and follow them now. They had to rescue Tawnee. How frightened she must be. To think what she must have seen in the village that day. It filled him with anger and vengeance. And where were their parents? If they were safe, they should have found them by now.

"How long have you been awake?" Kadya yawned. He was looking down the mountain with his back to her.

"A while," he replied, not looking at her.

"What is wrong?" she said, running her fingers through her hair and twisting it at the nape of her neck.

There was no easy way to tell her.

"I saw children from our village in the group. They may all be from our village."

He could not read the expression on her face.

"Who did you see?"

"I saw Latka and Mosi sleeping. I could not see all of them."

He could tell her concern was growing. He paused before delivering the news he dreaded.

"Tawnee is with them."

Kadya froze as every ounce of sleepiness left her body. She looked through him as though he were invisible.

"Tawnee is alive?"

"Yes, I only saw her briefly. She was sleeping. I did not want to wake anyone."

Tears spilled down her cheeks.

Suddenly, she stood up, dashing away her tears.

"What are we going to do? We must go to her!" she cried.

"We will, but we do not know why Tawnee is with them or how she got there. It will be better for her if we wait until we know more."

"How will we find out anything more, Ruark?" she argued. "Tawnee is with strangers in the valley. They make her walk long distances every day. She sleeps on the hard ground each night. It must be horrible for her!"

Her voice was pleading now. Ruark saw her helplessness.

"Tawnee is alive, Kadya, and she appears unharmed."

"We do not know that!" she retorted.

He waited. "It will be easier to get Tawnee back if we know more. Try to remember this."

She stared at him before glancing down into the valley. She walked to an outcropping to get a better view. He watched her crouch down and shield her eyes from the glare. Eventually, she gave up and slowly walked back to where he waited.

"What do they want from little children? Why our village?" She sat across from him. "What can we do?"

"We will follow them and watch. When the time is right, we will know what to do." He did not want to tell her what he had in mind.

They walked down the mountain resolved to stay close to Tawnee. Each lost in their thoughts and concerns.

When they reached the valley, they found the group had abandoned the campsite. They were still heading upriver.

Grassland stretched between them and the riverbank in the narrow, flat valley. Staying hidden was difficult. Ruark believed they would make better time traveling higher on the mountain, but the path was rocky and steep.

For most of the day they walked within the tree line out of sight until they came to the river in the evening. They nearly stumbled upon the group of children. To avoid being seen, they hid behind a small boulder and peeked out.

Tawnee was sitting on a rock, looking at her foot. She rubbed it. They watched her for several minutes. Was she in pain?

Kadya moved forward, but Ruark held her back.

"No!" he whispered. "They cannot know we are here."

"But she is hurt. We can not just sit here and watch."

Kadya sat down, eyes on her sister. "I have to find a way to help her."

Tall pine trees surrounded the camp in the grassy enclosure. They recognized the children playing in the shade nearby. Soon, Tawnee jumped up and ran to join them. She did not seem afraid. Kadya could not take her eyes off the scene. "Ruark, why are they keeping them?"

He did not know. After a few moments, he said, under his breath, "I am going to find out."

Ruark was sure of one thing. The men knew where they were. Ruark could not find Pak anywhere. He was probably following them.

He told Kadya the rest of his plan. She was not happy about it. She would have to stay hidden until he returned with Tawnee.

"What if something happens and we are separated?"

It was an obvious question that Ruark refused to answer. He simply would not risk putting her in more danger.

Later, the sky faded from aqua blue to purple and orange. They moved to a small indentation in the mountainside. It was a place where the rock jutted out offering protection for the night. They would not be able to build a fire.

Kadya was exhausted from the stress and helplessness she felt. It did not take long for her to fall asleep under the fir branches they gathered near the Malevo camp.

Ruark knew he was taking an enormous risk. He would need to get a few hours of sleep if he was going to manage his plan. He laid back against the hard ground and put his arms behind his head.

He awoke to Kadya's urgent whisper, "Ruark, wake up!"

He opened his eyes to an unfamiliar orange glow.

"Is it a fire?" Kadya asked.

Ruark jumped to his feet, alert and frightened for Tawnee. They must get to her. Instinctively, Kadya followed him through the path of brush and rocks.

They made it down the mountain quickly. When they got close to the camp, he saw the fires were out. The children were sleeping, but the men were not there.

The glow was not coming from the fires. It was coming from a small pile of supplies. It was the orange stone.

Chapter 6

The orange stone is for healing from disease and brokenness," Ruark whispered. They watched from behind a boulder surrounded by shrubs.

"I thought they could not see the stones," Kadya whispered back.

"I do not think they can. If they could, they would know we have two of them already. Something else is going on."

He had to go through with his risky plan. It would have been easier without Kadya. He explained what he had in mind. "Wait over there until I give you the signal."

She moved up the hillside. Ruark watched the sleeping group. He spotted Pak at the far end of the clearing. Where were the men?

Ruark looked for Tawnee. He moved closer. Then he heard a small cry from Kadya. He turned to see one of the men carrying her away. He ran toward her when a shadow flew at him. He dropped to the ground and rolled away from his attacker. Getting to his feet, he ran away through the brush, between boulders and bushes. He had no intention of being caught. He climbed higher up the mountain, far from the path. He ran until he was sure no one followed him. Hopefully, he could find a cave like they had found days before.

It was very dark on this side of the valley. He could not see the path in front of him. He let it sink in that he was alone. The men had taken Kadya. Why had he put her in danger? The only comfort he had was thinking that Kadya was now with Tawnee. He should have kept Kadya safe. Instead, he had led her straight into harm's way.

Leaning his head against the chill of the rock, he sat and closed his eyes, exhausted and discouraged. Sadness and disappointment filled him. He sobbed openly, letting the pain and loss of the past weeks overtake him. He wanted to scream but he dared not. He cried until there were no tears left. He did not remember falling into a deep sleep.

Reality took hold in the morning when he woke up. He remembered the events of the night before. Both of his sisters were now held captive in the valley. He needed to get to them and find out why.

He made his way to a safe lookout spot. From here, he could see the clearing. The men were sitting by the fire while the children slept. He could not see either of his sisters. He desperately needed to know where they were and if they were safe.

He decided to cross the river to watch. He would have to wait and see what they would do next. He gathered some sticks near the riverbank and built a fire downwind from the party. His hunger outweighed any risk he felt from the men. Besides, he felt confident he could outrun them if necessary. He had done it before.

He knelt to wash his face and drink. The cool water was refreshing but did nothing for his worry and despair.

Would there be an end to this nightmare? Would he ever see his parents again? More importantly, could he save his sisters?

"No harm will come to them."

His thoughts were interrupted. He looked up, wiping his eyes. It was Pak.

Ruark jumped to his feet, alert now, ready to defend himself from being captured.

"My father sent me to find you. He understands they are your sisters. That is all the younger one would say. The older one will not speak."

So Kadya was not talking or giving any information, at least not yet. Ruark hoped she would hold out and not say anything about the stones.

"My father admires you. He says you are brave and skilled," he said rigidly. He waited for Ruark to respond.

Ruark was surprised. He felt Pak did not share his father's opinion.

The stones were in his pack near the water between them. Ruark was aware of their nearness. If Pak could see them, he would take them for sure. Walking to his pack, Ruark casually reached for the bag and secured it around his waist.

Slowly, he stepped closer to Pak. Without expression, he asked, "Why do you hold them?"

Pak was defiant.

Ruark glared back. He did not have time to deal with Pak's arrogance. Hunger made him impatient. He brushed past Pak and stepped into the water to watch for trout. He grabbed one and flung it out of the water onto the golden sand. It lay there, writhing. He walked out of the water.

He shook his hands and stared back at Pak. "Tell me why you hold them?" he asked again.

Pak stared at him.

Ruark ignored him and squatted to quickly slit the side of the fish, allowing the guts to slide out. He left it lying on the rock while he took out the sticks he used for cooking. He placed the raw meat over the fire.

Without a word, Pak turned to go.

Ruark watched him disappear into the trees.

When the meat was ready, he held one of the sticks close to his mouth and blew on it. He ate heartily and wrapped the rest into the pack around his waist. He put his hands over the fire, relishing the warmth. He thought about his plight. He had to stay close to Kadya and Tawnee. He had to free them.

Then he thought of Pak's words. Why did Pak say no harm would come to them.?

Were they using the children to find the stones? That had to be the reason. And now Kadya was with them. She could see the stones. He had to trust that she would know what to do.

He needed help. If he could get to the village, he might find his parents or someone to help rescue his sisters. After they were safe, he could double back and try to get to the pink stone. He wrestled with this for a while before dousing the fire and headed in the direction of the village.

Chapter 7

Kadya ran to where the children were sleeping and found Tawnee. She woke with a dazed expression, like seeing someone in a dream. Tawnee reached for her. Kadya held her sister, allowing Tawnee to be the first to let go.

Kadya refused to look at her captors. They stood silent, watching the reunion. She promised herself she would not speak to them. She would not say anything she knew about the stones.

One of the men turned to walk away, saying something Kadya could not understand. The other man followed him.

She spoke soothingly to Tawnee to calm her and stop her tears.

"Tawnee, you are safe. I am here now," she whispered. "Ruark will help us. He is keeping watch over us."

Tawnee blinked. All she could say was, "They took her. They took Mother."

Kadya held Tawnee tightly once again. She desperately wanted to run away with Tawnee and risk everything to escape. Instead, she held her sister's hands and looked around.

The other children were sleeping, undisturbed. She wanted to know what happened in the village and what Tawnee experienced. She wanted to know what had happened to her dear mother.

Just then, one of the men brought over an animal skin and threw it on the ground. She did not acknowledge his action. She had slept uncomfortably for many nights. She would not accept his offer of comfort. These men and others were responsible for separating her family and destroying her village. She would not give them the satisfaction of complying with whatever they wanted from her or her sister. For now, it was best to get some sleep.

"Tawnee," she said softly, "we will talk tomorrow. Go back to sleep now.

Tawnee was comforted by her sister's presence. She finally relaxed into a peaceful sleep.

Kadya lay there looking at the starlit sky. In the morning, she would figure out what to do. Ruark was safe and somewhere nearby. It was her only comfort. She held tight to Tawnee's hand and fell asleep.

Chapter 8

Ruark found the village burned to the ground. Only charred debris remained, left by people fleeing for their lives.

Pak's words echoed in his mind. Everyone is gone.

"Where did they go?" he thought, looking at the devastation. What happened to his mother and father? It was chilling to think that if he and Kadya had been in the village on that terrible day, he would know.

Discouraged, he walked back into the forest and slumped against the trunk of a tree. There was no one to help him rescue Kadya and Tawnee. The weight of responsibility he felt for their safety was overwhelming. He would have to double back to find them again. After one last look at the remains of his village, he decided to cross the river and travel on the other side.

The days were uneventful, one after the other. Ruark took opportunities to rest and hunt. Moving was much easier without another person to be concerned for, but he wished Kadya was still with him. At least she was with Tawnee.

Luckily, it was summertime. But the valley would soon fill with snow. Ruark hoped to have his sisters and the stones safe before moving to lower ground where the winter would be less severe.

Quietly, he watched an elk to his left. It was a buck with large antlers. He was impressed by its size. It reminded him of hunting with this father. If only his father were with him now. He closed his eyes and imagined what his father might say to encourage him. What advice would he give? He let the thoughts run through his mind until he fell asleep. When he woke up, he was comforted and calm. The buck was gone.

The sunlight glistened on the shallow water while he walked along the river. He imagined his sisters' faces and what they were doing. Each morning, he evaluated how long he had traveled and thought about where they might be. He hoped his calculations were reasonable. When evening came, he searched for any sign of them.

After four days, he finally saw the fires across the river.

Chapter 9

Kadya woke up early. It had been five days since she arrived at the Malevo camp. Tawnee was by her side. The days were difficult. They roamed narrow caverns and walked across rocky terrain. At times, they could see for miles. They searched constantly for the stones. After a midday break, they were forced on the trail again, searching for anything brilliant or shiny. At night, before sleeping, they spoke of their parents and how Ruark would soon help them escape.

One night, Tawnee was frightened by the sound of wolves howling in the distance. They seemed to be coming closer. Tawnee was afraid they were coming for her and could not sleep.

Kadya whispered, "Do you want to hear a story?"

"Yes," Tawnee answered.

Kadya remembered the way their father told stories and began her story the same way.

"A long time ago, when you were too small to remember, Ruark was about your age. He was walking alone in the woods above the village when he heard whimpers coming from the undergrowth in the trees along the pathway. Ruark could not see anything at first. When he looked closer, he found three baby wolf pups cuddled together. He moved away and sat at a distance to watch. He waited until the sun was very low in the sky with no sign of the mother. He decided the pups were in danger of starvation and other predators, so he brought them back to the village."

"We gave them food and watched them play. Do you remember, Tawnee?'

Tawnee looked at her sister, anxious for her to continue, "No. Tell me more about the wolf pups."

Well, they grew fast. Ruark hunted rabbits for them, but Father said they needed to go to the woods to learn how to hunt for themselves. Finally, they grew so big, he and Ruark took them up the mountainside to say goodbye."

"Did he ever see them again?" Tawnee asked expectantly.

"Yes, he has seen them many times. They remember him. They come to Ruark when he holds out his open palm to them. I am sure they remember his scent and know he cared for them. As they turn to leave, they always look back at him before they walk away."

Tawnee lay quietly, listening for the wolves again. "I wonder if they are the same wolves."

Kadya responded thoughtfully, "I like to think they are, Tawnee."

"I am not afraid anymore," she said. She snuggled close to Kadya and closed her eyes.

***

In the morning the air was chilly. Careful not to disturb Tawnee, Kadya got up and threw some dry twigs into the coals. She blew on the ashes to reignite the fire.

She welcomed any warmth she could find.

The two men were having a conversation. She pretended to be intent on her task while she listened to what they were saying.

"What luck to have a child from the village find the orange stone. If only we could find another," Hatu smirked.

Durk answered, "We need to search elsewhere. The legend says they were scattered. The child will not find another stone here."

Hatu responded, "We can move when we get more supplies. Is it not strange how she can see the stone differently than you or me? It was a good move to take the children. The wise one said, 'A child will find the stone.'"

So, this is why they are using the children to find the stones, Kadya thought. Their stories told them to do it.

Until now, she had only spoken to Tawnee and the other children. She refused to talk to Hatu or Durk. They were close to her father's age but so different from him. Durk was quiet and reserved. He had a gentle face and a long braid down his back. Hatu was short with thin, wiry hair that hung about his shoulders. He had a temper and was willing to use it to intimidate the children when necessary. Some evenings after the children were asleep, Kadya listened to their conversations. Although she could not understand everything they said, she recognized the sound of camaraderie and humor between them, suggesting they were not dangerous. However, she was always cautious around them and remained watchful to ensure the children were safe.

Each morning, Hatu used a gruff voice and his wild gestures to let the children know the expectation. Their job each day was to search for the stones. If you do not search, you will not eat. Kadya thought it was an act designed to terrorize small children into submission.

Tawnee and the other children seemed adjusted to their new way of life. There seemed to be no real sense of urgency to their searching. It was a purposeful existence that had become woven into their lives.

Only once in the five days had anyone seen anything close to resembling a special stone. They found only a pile of tan-colored rocks amongst the shrubs. Hatu was agitated and made the children keep searching the area as if it was their fault, there was no stone.

"So, your sister found the orange stone," Pak smirked, plopping down beside her, interrupting her thoughts. He had finished setting out the rations of meat and wheat-grass biscuits for the children as he did each morning.

She moved away uncomfortably and averted her gaze. She had not yet spoken and was sending a strong message of her disapproval to all of them by her silence.

Pak jabbed her with more conversation, ignoring her silent protest. "Now she must find the others," he motioned toward the mountains.

Kadya sensed his greedy arrogance and kept her lips closed tightly. Inside, she raged against him. How dare they use the children this way?

He continued to bait her, "Perhaps she will see her parents again."

Kadya wanted to scream. Instead, she got up and moved to the other side of the circle near Tawnee.

Hatu and Durk often taunted the children with promises to see their parents to bribe them. The children were disappointed when there was no stone. Pak's thoughtless comments hurt them more. It was cruel.

She hoped he felt ignored when he got up and walked away.

Kadya would never adjust to this new life. She always thought about ways to escape.

She knew the men had the orange stone. She could see it glowing inside the knapsack. They had no idea she could see it. They could not see the stone's glow. They could only see the awed expression on the children's innocent faces to know which one to keep.

She thought about the history of the stones and all Ruark had told her. She did not want to compromise her ability to see them by doing something wrong. Only those with pure hearts could see them. Her motives for wanting the orange stone were pure. Ensuring the orange stone was safe with the others would be a good thing. Ruark told her no one could own them or benefit from their power unless they were willing to accept what they offered. That was different from possessing and controlling them for personal gain.

She wrestled with this today while she walked. She watched for any sign of another stone. She kept to herself as much as possible because if she were to find one, she would need to conceal it and keep it to herself. She was unsure how the other children might respond. Could she keep a secret from them? So far, she did not need to worry. There were no signs of a stone anywhere.

"I remember the day I found the orange stone," Tawnee had told her. "It was the day before you arrived. I saw it glow by the stream. I had never seen anything so beautiful. It was between a large boulder and a fallen tree trunk. Hatu made the other children move out of the way. He kept asking me about it over and over, until he found it. That night they gave me extra blankets and food. I wanted to see Mother, but I was too afraid to ask."

Kadya's heart broke for Tawnee. She considered telling her that not everyone could see the stones but decided against it. "Tawnee, if you see another stone or think you see one, do not act surprised or say anything.

Tell only me. We can get the stone together."

Tawnee leaned a bit closer and nodded, understanding Kadya's words.

Kadya planned to free them and get the orange stone somehow, if possible. But where was Ruark? Without him, how would they survive? Kadya counted on Ruark being near, watching over them.

After the long day of searching, they finished eating and sat around the fire exhausted. Tawnee returned from relieving herself in the woods. Her face was glowing.

"I saw Ruark!" she whispered after she sat next to Kadya. "He told me I must not tell anyone but to let you know he was near. He is looking for empathy. He said you would understand."

Tawnee did not know the word empathy and stumbled when she said it, but Kadya knew what she was saying.

"Yes, Tawnee. We must not let anyone know. Ruark is going to help us escape."

She squeezed Tawnee's hand gently to reassure her. They must not appear to be excited that Ruark was nearby. Tawnee squeezed her hand back in acknowledgment of their secret.

Ruark was watching them. Kadya understood that he was going to get to the pink stone. But more importantly, she knew they must be ready when the time was right.

Chapter 10

Ruark knew someone was following him. He sensed them close by. Yet, every time he looked, there was no one. After several minutes, he decided to double back on a different path.

Suddenly, he stopped cold. In the distance, he could see Pak. Silently, he crept toward him. Pak turned just as Ruark lunged, tackling him to the ground. They wrestled, struggling against each other. Pak challenged him, answering every move with strength and knowledge. Ruark found it necessary to use all the techniques he practiced in the village with his friends. Neither of them uttered a word. They went back and forth, grunting and groaning with every move.

Finally, Ruark pulled Pak onto his back. He moved swiftly to secure him in a hold. Their eyes locked on one another for what seemed an eternity. Just as Ruark's strength was about to give, Pak went limp and averted his gaze in defeat.

Ruark released him and stood, hiding his exhaustion. He watched Pak sit up and pull his knees to his chest. He brushed the dirt from his hands, eyes still on the ground.

Moments later, Pak stood. He walked away into the trees without saying a word.

Chapter 11

Each morning, Kadya washed in the river to wake up. Today, the silvery clouds showed brilliant pinks and oranges, promising a warm day.

She had not slept well. Throughout the night, wolves howled. Shadows swayed in the breeze. A thunderstorm scattered lightning across the horizon. She was worried about Ruark. He was in no danger from the wolves or the storm. But the thought of him alone and the possibility she might never see him again kept sleep far away.

She counted the tiny sticks she collected in the fold of her waistband. There were ten sticks for ten days of endless searching.

She found the stash of stones she collected the night before. She laid them in a design Tawnee could identify. If one of them was a close enough match, Tawnee would bring it to her later. It was risky to exchange the orange stone with a fake, but Kadya would seize the opportunity when she got the chance.

She was about to walk into the clearing to find Tawnee when she noticed two strange men walking toward the camp. They carried several knapsacks and dragged a large pack behind them. They stared at her. Quickly, she moved into the shadows behind a tree and watched them greet Hatu and Durk. Durk stood and grabbed the taller one with a hearty laugh. Hatu opened the knapsacks and placed the contents in a pile of supplies.

So, this is how they stayed supplied with food.

She watched Durk. He sat by the fire with the younger men. They laughed and gestured in her direction. When she returned, she avoided eye contact and ignored them.

Kadya still refused to speak to Hatu and Durk. At times, she thought they were becoming impatient with her. However, they recognized her role with the children. She kept them calm and cared for them.

She joined them now and waited for them to wake up.

Latka and Mosi were brothers. They were a year older than Tawnee. Mica was a year younger. Dala and Rori were the same age. They were sister and brother. Little Ari was the youngest.

Tawnee rubbed her eyes and swiped the long, tangled locks away from her face.

"I saw Mother in my dream," she said with a yawn. "I ran to her. But when I reached her, I woke up."

She looked younger than her seven years.

Kadya thought the children were very brave. Each mourned their loss privately and seemed resigned to their new life. At what point would they simply forget they had mothers and fathers?

"They didn't give us anything to eat if we cried," Tawnee said one night. "They told us we would never see our mothers again if we didn't keep searching."

Kadya realized she was like them, forced to forget her parents or the pain would paralyze her, and she would not survive.

To pass time, Kadya recalled the stones' locations to try to find a pattern. The blue stone was high on a hillside in a cave. Days later, they found the yellow stone behind a waterfall. Tawnee found the orange stone along a creek bed in a gorge far from the others. The pink stone was high on a cliff, unreachable. There was no pattern she could recognize.

So why did the men change directions on the ninth day and cross to the other side of the river? It seemed they were traveling in circles. It did not make sense. She was growing uneasy. She could not shake the feeling that things were about to change. Her deepest fear was separation from Tawnee. She could not bear the thought.

Following the river gave Kadya a reasonable knowledge of their location. If she was correct, the village was at least a two or three-day walk. It they could make it there they would have food. She and her mother had stored plenty of dried meat, berries, grains, and vegetables in the dugout on the hillside. Hopefully, it was not found by the intruders on the day of the attack. If they could make it that far, they could wait for Ruark to find them. He would understand. She would risk everything to run away if only she knew how to take Tawnee and the children with her.

Chapter 12

Ruark stood at the edge of the cliff. He had climbed since early morning. The sun was directly overhead. Here, the land was barren except for a few boulders and withered shrubs. Sparse huddles of grass strained in the fierce and constant wind, struggling to thrive in the brief summer growing season.

There would be no way to get to the pink stone when the winter snows came. Ruark hoped he and his sisters would be together then, far to the south. He missed them. He longed to know they were okay.

He sat behind a large rock to shield himself from the wind and eat his rations. He needed time to think. Reaching the stone would be difficult. Here on top of the cliff, he understood how dangerous it was. He might not be able to do it alone.

Someone placed the stone there long ago. There must be a way to get to it. Who put it there, high on the side of the cliff? Why was it so difficult to reach? These troubling questions occupied his waking thoughts and harassed his dreams. Who decided what the stones should offer? Where did the idea begin? Why could some people see them and others not?

He hoped for answers, but none came.

After his meal, Ruark surveyed the edge of the cliff. He laid flat on his stomach to peer down into the vastness of the valley. He found places he could climb if he dared. First, he would have to know the precise location of the stone. It was out of view, but hopefully, he could see its glow in the darkness. He needed to be off the mountain by evening. Spending the night in the cold desolation of the mountaintop was risky.

The river snaked below with a silver light in the afternoon sun. He began his descent. He saw storm clouds building in the west. He did not want to get caught in a downpour. His father had taught him to be wary of lighting and wind high on a mountain.

He walked past the various landmarks he had identified earlier. He saw the huge rock resembling the shape of a face, a patch of burned trees, and a stream-lined with boulders strewn between the hillsides. He followed downstream as the valley fell out of sight. He would emerge by the river at dusk.

He came to a narrow stand of tall pines. He noticed something he had missed before. A crude shelter made with branches and logs. It surrounded the tree trunks near the forest floor. He worked his way closer, cautious of who might be hiding there. He stopped to listen but could only hear is own labored breathing.

He peered into the opening at the dirt floor of the forest. Crawling inside, he could barely stand under the makeshift covering of the roof. It appeared abandoned.

As he emerged into the shadows and made his way toward the stream, he kept watch for anyone nearby. He noticed footprints. They were barely visible, but one dragged behind the other, suggesting injury or lameness. The only person he encountered in the past several days was Pak. The thought of someone else was unsettling. He would have to stay hidden.

When Ruark came to the river's edge, it was early evening. He crossed the rushing river on exposed boulders until he found a shallow place to drink. The cold water felt good. He took the opportunity to sit and rest, allowing the water to rush around him. He would hunt and find a place to stay for the night.

He walked further and noticed an opening to a small gorge covered in trees and brush. A brook gushed in the distance. It was a perfect place to build a fire. Little sunlight penetrated here, and the evening shadows made it difficult to see. But he could see the cliffside.

He hid behind some bushes to wait for any small game to pass by. The long climb wore him out. He was famished. Luckily, he did not have long to wait. His bow was ready, and he released it. Soon, he watched the fire sizzle beneath the dripping grouse he had gutted and cleaned. The familiar scent made his mouth water.

He remembered learning to make a fire when he was young. His father made it look easy. He encouraged him as he struggled, confident in his ability. Ruark had finally mastered the art and could do it skillfully.

The thought of his father seared his heart. If only he were here. Tears welled in his eyes. He was discouraged. Somehow, he and his sisters must survive the destruction that had closed in around them. Despair was no use. He had to find answers. The morning sun would bring him closer to a solution. Meanwhile, the pink glow across the valley gave him hope.

Chapter 13

Kadya's eyes shot open from a deep sleep in the early dawn. She twisted to escape, but the arms were too strong. She struggled as tears burned in her eyes, resisting the urge to scream. She did not want to frighten the children.

After pulling her away from the camp, her captor squatted down to whisper in her ear, "You are coming with us. We are not going to hurt you."

She tried to free herself and run away, but it was useless. Either way, Tawnee was left alone. She had been right to fear the two young men when they arrived at the camp the day before.

Terrified, she stopped struggling. "My sister, bring my sister, too," she pleaded. She looked into his eyes, appealing to any kindness or understanding he might have, but it was no use. He ignored her words and pushed her forward, walking behind her.

Instinctively, she ran in the direction of the trees, dodging small bushes and fallen branches. She did not care. She would keep running forever to be with Tawnee again. Frantically, she looked for a place to hide until she felt him grab her arms from behind. He held her tightly against him.

He whispered hoarsely, "We are taking you to our village. It will be better for you there." After a brief pause, he repeated, "We are not going to hurt you."

She felt the energy drain from her body. She was helpless.

He gripped her wrist and pinned it behind her back. "Go," he said. She shook her arm, trying to release it, but he gripped it tighter.

He marched her out of the trees where the other man waited on the path. He was preparing the remaining supplies they would need for their return trip to their village.

Defiantly, she pulled away from her captor, which he allowed. He stayed right behind her, which enraged her even more.

Kadya walked between them, desperate to escape. What about Tawnee? She would soon wake up and find herself alone. To abandon her again was too much. Angry tears filled her eyes. She was determined to run away and get back to her. It was still early. The morning light was just beginning to show. She would use shadows to tell the time of day and remember every visual landmark to remember her location. She must stay aware of their direction and how far they traveled.

The men spoke in words she could not understand. Were they following orders given to them by Hatu and Durk back at camp? What did they want with her?

When they stopped along the bank of the river, Kadya found a place away from them. It jutted out above the water. She stared into the rippling water at the sunlit pebbles, planning her escape.

She did not know how long she could remain silent, but she was determined not to cooperate. She would wait for her opportunity.

The shorter of the two men got up and walked toward her. Kadya stiffened. He handed her some dried meat. She looked at him blankly before turning her head away in refusal.

"You need to eat," he said sternly, nudging her elbow. "We have a long journey ahead."

Kadya ignored him and continued looking away. Finally, he dropped the meat on the rock and stomped away impatiently.

Grudgingly, she picked up the meat and began to eat. They watched her. She took little comfort in the words "they would not hurt her" and knew she should not push them too far. For now, she was at the mercy of these strangers.

By the time she finished, they were ready to go. Reluctantly, she joined them. She had no choice.

All afternoon, she thought of Tawnee. If Ruark was close by, he would know Tawnee was alone. It brought her small comfort. She looked for landmarks and any sign they were close to her village. She remembered how the river looked near her old home. How many times had she and her mother gone to get water? Something would look familiar to her. At the right time, she would get away to the food storage chamber up the mountainside. It was well hidden. Once she was there, she would have everything she needed.

The sun sank lower in the sky. Kadya was grateful for the cooling effect as it dipped behind the mountain. When the men were ready to set up camp for the night, she was eager to be left alone. She sat at a distance and watched them organize supplies. She wondered how long they spent traveling between their village and the group searching for the stones.

"What is your name?"

Kadya was startled by the question, not wanting to reveal it. But what did it matter now?

"Kadya," she stammered.

"Kadya," he repeated.

"I am Raffi." He turned back to his preparations.

She sat there in awkward silence.

"That is Tarek," Raffi said casually.

Tarek walked into the clearing carrying a large bird flung over his shoulder. He threw it on the ground. Raffi jumped into action, eager to clean the bird and get it cooked. Tarek looked at her coolly and walked away. He was tall with dark eyes that looked straight through her. His hair fell down his back, tied with a piece of hide. It was his strong arms that had grabbed her that morning.

"His uncle is Durk," Raffi offered.

Kadya did not care and looked away.

The scent of cooking meat filled the air. It made Kadya hungry. They ate it with boiled sweet potato, and the mushrooms Raffi had gathered earlier that day.

When she finished eating, she rose to leave the men to find a place to sleep and be alone.

"I suppose you want to know why we took you from the others," Tarek said.

She stood quietly, looking back at him without expression.

He motioned for her to join them at the fire. At first, she hesitated, unsure she should let her guard down. Then, she sat and waited to hear what he had to say.

"My uncle has been watching you and says you are older than your years and brave. He is also impressed by your brother. He says he is very skilled and wise."

Kadya did not comprehend his words. What did any of this have to do with taking her from Tawnee? She struggled to remain calm. Her anger flared remembering how violently she was ripped away. She fought for self-control, betraying nothing.

Tarek continued, "He asked us to bring you back to our leader as a gift. He says you would make an excellent wife for his son."

Wife. Gift. The horror unfolded in her mind. She knew what it meant.

There were marriages in her village, too, but no one was taken against their will to become the wife of their leader's son. Her resolve to escape grew stronger with each passing moment. Unable to stand their presence any longer, she got up to find a place to lie down away from the fire.

In the chilly air, she watched them as anxious thoughts spiraled through her head. She noticed an orange glow coming from one of their packs. Raffi and Tarek were bringing the orange stone back to their village.

She closed her eyes. The orange stone would not be lost after all.

Chapter 14

The morning sun was bright. Ruark was feeling confident. During the night, he decided to bring Kadya and Tawnee to the abandoned shelter. There, they could stay hidden and far from danger. They would also have the time they needed to get the pink stone. He crossed the river.

He was eager to retrace his steps to find any sign of the person responsible for building it. He crept silently, stopping a distance away from the shelter to watch and wait. Birds sang in the trees above him. The sounds of the forest seemed uninterrupted by his presence. The air was still in the tall pines that towered above him with their dense trunks buried in the moist brown dirt. There was no undergrowth. The ground around him was dark and cool. It was a relief from the earlier heat.

He observed the animals that wandered by, aware of every sound and movement around him. They reminded him of his father's words. "Son, learn from our animal brothers and sisters. They have much to teach us." Ruark had been younger then and did not understand. But now, he carefully watched the animals' alertness to predators and awareness of danger. Today, he watched them enter the area and recognize his presence, raising their heads to catch the unfamiliar scent. Some edged closer out of curiosity, while others bounded away in fear at the intrusion of their quiet and untouched environment. It occurred to him there might be more to learn from them.

Satisfied the shelter was unoccupied, he decided to stay for the night. He needed to be well rested. It was two days of travel before he could find Kadya and Tawnee. Before dark, he went to the stream to fill his waterskin. He had just enough leftover meat to get through the night.

When he woke at sunrise, he was ready for the journey. He picked some berries and let the sweet juices linger in his mouth. He would fish a couple hours upriver.

Meanwhile, he traveled at the edge of the forest in the cool shade of the canopy. There would be plenty of time to rescue his sisters and secure the pink stone with their help.

Chapter 15

Ruark stood behind an outcropping. To his great relief, he could see two fires. He had followed them since early afternoon. The children and their captors, Hatu and Durk, wandered up the side of the mountain and back down, searching in vain for stones along the stream bed. They were farther upriver than Ruark expected they would be, heading in the opposite direction of the shelter and the pink stone.

He watched the valley below. His sisters were down there and tonight, he would steal them away. It would be perilous. The two men would surely try to recapture them, because they could see the stones. But Ruark had to take the chance. If they could make it back to the cave where they found the blue stone, they could hide. Now, he needed to get to the campsite and position himself to get their attention. It all depended on getting one of them alone and telling them it was time. He had to be careful. Pak would be watching.

Slowly, he made his way close enough to see the faces of the children around the fire. Tawnee was sitting alone. She stared blankly into the flames. He searched for Kadya but could not find her. Where could she be?

He waited. Some of the children played games together while Tawnee sat silently. One of the men came over and spoke to her briefly. Tawnee did not look at him or respond.

Something was wrong. *Where was Kadya?* Ruark looked on with mounting fear. He had to think of something fast.

Tawnee stood and walked out of the clearing toward the forest. Ruark moved quickly to get to Tawnee in time.

She turned with a terrified look on her face, but relaxed when she recognized her brother.

"Come with me," Ruark whispered.

Tawnee looked back at the group through the trees afraid they were watching for her to return. She looked back at Ruark in desperation.

"They took Kadya away," she cried. Tears filled her eyes.

"Come with me, now!" he said urgently, "There is no time. You never have to be here again. We will be together. We will find Kadya!"

She took his hand as he whisked her off the path. They ran through the brush up the side of the mountain, climbing higher and higher in the darkness. Tawnee flew behind Ruark as he pulled her along.

It was too early to tell if they were followed. Soon enough, the men in the camp would realize Tawnee was missing and go in search of her. He wanted to stop and ask about Kadya, but he did not dare.

They moved quickly, slowing only when they rounded a boulder or clump of trees. When they were far enough away, Ruark stopped and held Tawnee in a tight embrace.

"Tawnee, I am so glad you are safe. They have not hurt you, have they?"

He held her back to look her up and down, trying to find any signs of harm. She shook her head sadly.

"They took Kadya," she said helplessly with a vacant look. She held out Kadya's hairpin.

Ruark took it and got to his knees.

"Who took Kadya?"

"Two men. They came to bring supplies. When they left, they took Kadya with them. I saw them drag her away." Tawnee began to cry.

Ruark held his younger sister close. A sinking feeling of hopelessness settled into his stomach. He placed the hairpin in his pack with the stones.

"We must get far away from here. We will find a way to get Kadya, but now, we must run from here. Do you understand?"

Tawnee nodded.

He continued, "We need to get as far as we can before morning."

She nodded again. The hopeless look in her eyes broke Ruark's heart.

They hiked in silence and reached the cave at dawn. Ruark knew there was a possibility Pak followed them, but Tawnee needed to rest. He hoped the men were going in a different direction and might not bother to chase them.

They went as deep into the cave as they could go. There was no light. Although the opening soared above them, the cave ceiling was low inside. They had to crawl on their knees to go further. The cave turned to the left, offering the security of darkness. Ruark could not see Tawnee, so he held tightly to her hand. She clung to him in silence.

"We will sleep here for a while. Then we must keep

going." He helped her find a place to lie down and leaned against the rough cave wall.

Exhausted, Tawnee fell asleep, holding fast to Ruark's leg.

Ruark drifted to sleep, his dreams haunted by Kadya's screams. He watched helplessly as his mother's eyes filled with terror. Smoke and flames choked out their village. The form of his father loomed above him, dark eyes piercing through him for an answer Ruark did not know.

He was jarred awake by a sound inside the cave. Reality engulfed him, suffocated him, erasing the clarity of the faces he loved so much from his dreams.

He listened in the darkness.

If it was one of the men, they might think to light a fire. His back stiffened against the wall. His heartbeat pounded in his ears. He hoped Tawnee would not wake up.

The sound of footsteps came closer. His mind raced for a way to escape. He could feel the presence of someone nearby. They would have to crawl if they came any closer. He held his breath, waiting for the worst. Suddenly, they made a whistling sound and walked toward the cave opening.

Ruark did not move a muscle. If Tawnee woke up, she might make a sound to alert the intruder. The waiting was unbearable.

Slowly, he loosened Tawnee's arm from his leg and eased himself around the curve of the wall to look toward the lighted entrance of the cave. It must be mid-morning by now. He stopped short to see the outline of Pak, sitting at the opening of the cave, looking out. Did he know they were there? Was he waiting, knowing they were trapped?

Ruark grew increasingly impatient. What could Pak do? He could not force them to go back. Ruark was not going to let him take Tawnee. What did he have to gain by sitting there?

He toyed with the idea of another wrestling match, only this time, he would make sure Pak could not walk away.

Tawnee turned and repositioned herself, fast asleep. He prepared himself for the inevitable, but she did not wake up. He turned to watch Pak again and waited.

Finally, Pak left the cave. Ruark cautioned himself to wait. Pak could still be watching from a distance.

After several agonizing hours, Tawnee woke up and called out his name.

"I am here. We must stay quiet. Pak followed us. I think he is gone now."

Tawnee sat up but stayed quiet.

"Wait here, I will be right back," he said.

He walked toward the brilliant daylight, forcing his eyes to adjust. He peered down the rocky hillside. Here, at the cave opening, the path narrowed and formed a ledge above a sloping meadow. To the right, the trail continued up a steep incline.

He could see no sign of anyone. Lying on his stomach, he pulled himself closer to the edge. If Pak had discovered them, he could be watching from the trees.

Pak could not force them to do anything. They had escaped. Tawnee was free from the grueling days of wandering in search of the stones.

The thought of Kadya missing made him twinge. She must be days away by now, traveling who knows where.

Thinking of what she was going through was overwhelming. Ruark could only deal with the present moment and get Tawnee as far away as possible. Giving in to never seeing Kadya again was not an option.

He would deal with Pak if necessary. He walked back into the darkness of the cave. "Tawnee, we need to go," he called softly.

A much-disheveled Tawnee emerged into the daylight. Her long hair was tangled and hiding her eyes. Her dress showed the wrinkles from sleeping on the cave floor. Brushing the hair away, she looked at Ruark with disbelief, unsure if it was safe to come out.

"Pak was here, but he is gone now. If he comes back, he cannot take you with him. You are safe with me now," he reassured her.

"What about Kadya?" she asked intently, her eyes pleading.

"We will make a plan to find her," he replied, suppressing his doubts. "She is strong. Come on. We need to get far away from here. We are still too close. We must find food and keep going."

Ruark took her hand and guided her down the trail where they could drink from the river and hopefully catch some food. He worried about Tawnee. She seemed so frail. Her eyes appeared enormous against her sunken cheeks. She was in desperate need of nourishment and rest.

The late morning sun sparkled across the tall grass spotted with wildflowers. On any other day, before the attack, they would have played games and picked flowers for their mother. But those days were gone, he thought bitterly. Now, they had to survive on their own.

"Ruark, look!" Tawnee pointed. She ran toward the edge of the forest. Alarm shot through him. He thought she had seen Pak. Instead, he found her pulling plump blackberries off the branches one by one and stuffing them into her mouth.

Her smile surprised him. She had been through so much. He was relieved for a chance to relax. He smiled back and followed her lead for breakfast.

Chapter 16

Kadya could see the orange stone next to Tarek, in his pack. The pulsing orange glow reassured her. She listened to the familiar joking of the men. This morning, their laughter had jolted her awake. She feigned sleep to hear more of their plans.

When she got up, Tarek watched her walk to the river.

They had passed her family's village days ago. She no longer recognized places along the river. Now, she kept track of landforms and markers for her eventual escape.

There had been no chance to get away, and time was running out to get the orange stone. Tarek carried it in his waist pack and only took it off in the evening. He rarely left it long enough for her to have the opportunity. The stones she carried to replace it were tied in the skirt of her dress. She hoped one of the stones would resemble the orange stone enough to fool them.

She had barely spoken to them in days. She gave little cooperation beyond eating and staying between them on the trail. Sometimes, she remembered Tawnee's laughter or Ruark's reassuring voice to keep her sanity.

Last night, she overheard they would be at their village the following day. Kadya was desperate to run away with or without the stone. The thought of being forced to marry a stranger filled her with terror.

She knew Tarek and Raffi were tired of her silence, but she did not want to reveal anything to them. Tarek often asked if she was hungry or if she needed to stop and rest. The only reason she could imagine for his kindness was that she was valuable to them for their leader. It angered her to think they might receive a reward for bringing her as a prize.

They would be disappointed, she vowed. Because Kadya would make sure she was far away from here and in the safety of the life she had known. Tonight was her last chance. She would take the stone and go back to her village. She would stay in the storage cave until Ruark came for her.

When she returned from the river, Tarek was waiting to hand her some dried meat and a water-filled skin. He held it and moved her hair out of the way. Kadya was startled at this gesture and froze in place. Their eyes met briefly. He was uncomfortably close, and she looked away. She did not want to betray her fear.

"Why do you look away?" he asked pointedly.

She wanted to scream at him and tell him he had taken everything from her. Instead, she buried the scream in silence and gazed at him sullenly, with all the emotion she could muster.

Tarek turned away. Perhaps he did not want to look into the eyes of someone who had suffered so much. He looked back only to see if she was following them as they started their day's journey.

They walked until the sun was overhead. She wanted

to rest. The stones under her garment were hitting her leg. She was sure there was a bruise to show for it. She longed to remove them.

The river was wide and shallow. The clear water glittered in the late morning sunlight. Tarek and Raffi examined the ground for tracks near the river's edge. They knew this place well since it was a day from their home. Kadya was glad they wanted to stop. It was unlikely that any large game would be at the river in the middle of the day. Most drank at sunrise and sunset.

She was surprised to see Raffi positioning his bow. In his usual joking manner, he challenged Tarek to a match. They chose a narrow birch tree on the other side of the river as the target. Each took a turn releasing their arrows. Raffi's arrow missed. Tarek's hit the tree and bounced off. Raffi's next arrow penetrated the tree. Tarek's arrow missed completely.

Tarek stopped for a moment to reposition. He put down his bow and untied the waist pack, dropping it to the ground.

Kadya eyed the pack. This was her opportunity to exchange the stones. If only Tarek and Raffi could be distracted long enough by their game. Perhaps she could distract them more. She was skilled with a bow. Her father had encouraged her to learn even though hunting was the role of the men in the village. In the days before the attack, she and Ruark shot together for hours at a time. Her father only recently presented her with a bow of her own. Unfortunately, she had left it behind on the day of the attack.

While Raffi was aiming his next shot, she gathered all her courage and walked up behind Tarek. He turned, caught off guard by her nearness. Without saying a word, she reached for the bow in his hand.

Their eyes met. Tarek smiled slightly and handed her the bow. He reached for an arrow and gave it to her. The bow was heavier than she imagined, but she stood straight and allowed herself time to adjust to the weight and reposition her feet. Slowly, she set it, her eyes squinting at the target.

She let it fly, watching it bounce off the tree right below Raffi's arrow. Raffi and Tarek stared at each other and then offered her another. She hit the tree again.

They laughed, asking her to join in their challenge. They shot arrow after arrow, laughing at their misses and shaking their heads at Kadya's accuracy.

In the end only one of her shots missed the tree.

Kadya played along in their game until all the arrows were across the river. Her arm ached. She would be sore for a few days. It had taken all her strength.

As Raffi and Tarek crossed the river, she stayed behind. It was now or never to get the stone.

She sat in front of Tarek's waist pack laying in the sand. She watched the two men wade through the nearly waist-deep water. Quickly, she reached into the waist pack directly behind her, careful to hold her other hand still in her lap.

She felt for the stone and found it. It was similar in size to the two stones she carried. When she saw it, the orange glow made her hesitate. The brilliance was so obvious. How could they not see it?

For a moment, she worried Tarek would look in her direction, but he was too concerned with finding and counting his arrows on the other shoreline. She hastily placed the stone under her dress. Next, she had to unbind the two stones she was carrying. A knot held them in the underside of her dress. She tried to untie them, but using one hand was not working. Her heart raced as she fumbled to untie it.

At last, she was able to release the stones and make the replacement. It was not an exact match, but she hoped the men had not inspected it too closely and were only concerned with getting it delivered. By the time they got it to their village, she planned to be far away.

Her next task was to get the replacement back into Tarek's waist pack before they returned from across the river. She reached into the waist pack to place the stone where Tarek would not notice it had been disturbed.

She checked again to see if the men were watching. Time was running out. Finally, she had to secure the orange stone into her dress without being obvious. With no time to lose, she dropped the stone through the opening at her neck and hoped to move it later.

When they came back across the river, she stood, secretly pushing the extra stone into the sand with her foot while the orange stone slipped lower toward her waist.

She watched them return with the same somber expression they were accustomed to while they gathered their supplies. She held her breath as Tarek fastened his waist pack, feeling for the stone inside. What if he noticed a difference? Relief flooded through her as Tarek began organizing the rest of his items.

Although they watched her carefully, she knew they were always agreeable to her need for privacy. Once hidden in the trees, she dislodged the orange stone from her dress. It fell to the ground, glowing brilliantly. Fighting the urge to run away, she quickly secured it in a knot under her skirt before emerging from the trees, prepared for the next phase of her plan. She would run away tonight.

Chapter 17

Ruark and Tawnee walked all day toward the wooded gorge where Ruark stayed before. He hoped to reach it before dark so they could eat and rest.

They talked about searching for the stones and finding Kadya. Hiding his fears, Ruark decided to tell Tawnee all he could remember about the stones to help distract her from her sadness.

"The stones belonged to a brother and a sister," he began. "It was along ago when everything was new. Their father entrusted the stones to them before he died. Everyone could see the stones then. This is how the trouble began."

Ruark wanted to tell the story like his father had told it to him.

"What trouble?" Tawnee asked. She listened carefully to understand the story as they walked along a narrow, wooded path.

"Before things went wrong, the stones were in a secret place, high on a mountain. Each year, seven days before the longest day, the council brought them down from the mountain. The people would get to see the stones. Each day, they honored a different stone to remember all they received from its offering. They waited for the final day when the most beautiful stone was brought out. They feasted on that day. Each person vowed to live by what the stones offered. This is how it was from the beginning."

Tawnee stopped him. "What do you mean about the different stones and their offerings?

"Well," he explained, "the stones have powers to offer those who can see them."

"What kind of powers?" Tawnee asked, intrigued by what her brother was saying.

Ruark spoke slowly. He listed them aloud, "Peace, healing, courage, empathy, abundance, wisdom, and harmony."

"Which stone did I find, the orange one?" she asked eagerly.

"The orange stone offers healing."

"Healing from sickness?"

"Yes, to those who accept it," Ruark replied.

Talking while they walked made them forget their weariness.

"Tell me about the other stones. How did you find them?" Tawnee urged. "I can see them but what do they offer?"

He led her to a grassy area surrounded by trees, protecting them from the heat of the late afternoon sun. Motioning for her to sit down, Ruark sat across from his sister and untied his waist pack to reveal the stones. He laid them on the grass.

"Kadya and I found the blue stone first, in a cave wall soon after the attack. It stands for peace and tranquility. This yellow stone was behind a waterfall. It offers abundance. Abundance means having plenty," he explained.

"You said we would see the pink stone soon," she

interjected. "What does it mean?"

"The pink stone offers empathy," Ruark said with a nod, "the ability to see from someone else's point of view and feel what they feel."

Tawnee thought for a moment. "That is only four of the stones. Why were they scattered? What caused the trouble?"

Ruark sighed and continued his tale. "As I said, in the beginning all was well. Everyone could see the stones. One day the father took his son and daughter to the secret place where the stones were kept. He held each glowing stone one by one, instructing them to take what each of the stones offered and hold them as most valuable. By doing so, they would receive the stone's offerings. He warned them to stay pure in their hearts and never lose sight of the stones. After he died, they grew older. They began to distrust each other. The village watched them grow more and more embittered. People took sides and were not satisfied to keep the stones in their special place. They wanted them for themselves. When they went to find the stones, they could not find them because they could not see them. After that, the stones were gone. Somehow, they were scattered."

He gathered the stones up and placed them in his pack.

"No one knows what happened?"

"No," he smiled gently. "Let's talk of it later. We need to find a place to make camp for the night."

Tawnee followed him. They walked in silence absorbed in their thoughts.

"We should be able to see the pink stone any moment now," Ruark said as they rounded the bend in the river that brought the cliff into view. There, high on the cliffside, was a glittering pink light.

Tawnee was the first to see it. "Tell me again what it means," she said breathlessly, eyes fixed on the view.

"Empathy," Ruark repeated quietly, "the ability to see from someone else's point of view. To be able to feel what they feel."

She looked down. "If those men had empathy, they would not have taken Kadya."

"Yes," Ruark answered. "They would not have attacked our village."

After a supper of berries and trout, Tawnee asked, "Will we stay here?"

"We could, but I have another place I want to show you on the other side of the river. Tomorrow, we will go across. Now we should sleep."

Ruark lay there unable to sleep. He had to think of something. His reasons for taking Tawnee to the shelter were twofold. He wanted to keep Tawnee safe, and he wanted to find a way to the pink stone. But he also had to decide what to do about Kadya. Likely, she was moving farther and farther away each day.

The pink light shimmered high above them far out of reach. He had to think of something.

Chapter 18

Kadya was frantic to escape as they left the openness of the sunlit valley and walked into the forested hillside. Tall trees cast a cool shadow. It was difficult for her eyes to adjust. She looked around at the small huts made of sticks with rawhide tied across them.

They had reached the village sooner than she expected. People were everywhere, cheering noisily and yelling. Everyone gathered to welcome Raffi and Tarek home. They stared at Kadya with curiosity.

Kadya took deep breaths, trying to remain calm. She was unsure of what was happening and very much aware of the orange stone nestled against her leg. What if someone was able to see it?

Tarek put his hand on her elbow to guide her through the crowd, leaving Raffi to deal with the welcoming throng.

Kadya's concern mounted with every step. Where was he taking her?

They stopped in front of a lodge that marked the end of the pathway. A boy about her age was sitting beside the opening, sharpening arrows. He rose to greet Tarek.

They exchanged words Kadya did not understand. After several minutes, a woman came out from behind the rawhide doorway.

The woman and Tarek spoke in quiet tones. She neither smiled nor looked at Kadya. She listened intently to Tarek with seeming dissatisfaction. Then, she disappeared into the lodge.

Kadya felt Tarek's gaze. He seemed uneasy. They had barely spoken for days. Perhaps he was having doubts.

The woman emerged from the lodge. She mumbled something to Tarek. He looked at Kadya and said, "You must go with her now." His voice was strained.

Kadya looked away. She did not want him to see her tears. She had lost everything. Her life would never be the same. He had been kind despite her punishing silence. She wanted to plead with him and beg him to help her. But why would he? He was going to receive a reward for bringing her here. He could not possibly care what happened to her.

He turned and walked away, which hurt her more. Kadya was sure she would never see him again.

The woman watched her without expression and groaned aloud. She beckoned Kadya to follow her down a stone pathway that led behind the lodge and up the mountainside. Here was another smaller hut covered in vines from the surrounding trees, making it almost invisible. The woman did not speak but stopped at the opening, gesturing for Kadya to go inside. Kadya looked at her with growing reservation.

She had to crouch low to avoid bumping her head. She stepped down into a room that was larger than she expected it to be. A small fire burned in the center, venting smoke through an opening in the roof. There was little light due to the heavy forest surrounding the hut. It was hard to see in the dim firelight.

Kadya expected to be alone. She was surprised to find a girl sitting on the floor, weaving grass into a mat. The girl ignored her until she made a final knot and laid down her work. Then she stood and walked to Kadya, bowing before her without speaking. She did not smile, but her soft eyes reflected the firelight.

She placed her fingers on her chest and said, "Pita."

Pita must be her name.

Kadya did not speak but acknowledged the girl with a slow nod.

Pita took Kadya's elbow and turned her toward a small sleeping cot along the wall near the fire. She motioned for Kadya to sit down, then knelt before her. She reached for Kadya's feet.

Kadya, suddenly aware of the stone now lodged against the inside of her knees and its proximity to the girl's face, moved her foot aside in a quick motion.

Pita stood up and quickly apologized. Kadya saw the fear in her eyes and something else, too, that she could not identify.

Kadya was unsure what to do. Pita gestured toward the cot and motioned for her to put her feet up. Kadya realized she wanted her to lie down and rest.

Without taking off her sandals, she leaned back and pulled her legs up under her, careful to keep the stone protected and out of view.

Pita went to her place on the floor next to her weaving and became absorbed in her work.

Could Pita see the stone?

Kadya closed her eyes and pretended to sleep. She

needed time to think. She would have to cooperate until the time to escape presented itself. She slipped into a restless slumber.

The smell of something cooking brought her back to reality. She woke to find Pita crouched by the fire, slowly stirring a pot. The delicious scent reminded her of the soup her mother made. She felt hungry for the first time in days.

"I need to go outside," Kadya said. Pita directed her to the back of the hut and showed her a large pot. Kadya understood what she expected her to do but felt uncomfortable. She longed to be out in the fresh air to find a stream to wash her face and hands, but she knew the girl would not allow it. So, she sat on the edge of the cot and reviewed her surroundings. The room in the hut was barren except for a few possessions along the wall, which she guessed belonged to Pita.

Pita carried a small bowl of steaming broth and handed it to Kadya. "Eat."

Kadya was grateful for the warm meal which reminded her of home.

The older woman came in shouting orders. Pita nervously straightened the room and retrieved the pot Kadya used earlier. The woman stopped Pita as she walked to the door and slapped her across the face.

Kadya was stunned at her cruelty.

Pita took the pot outside and left Kadya alone with the woman staring at her from across the room.

"Come here," she commanded.

Kadya resolved not to comply with her wishes. She was going to run away. This woman would not be able to stop her. Her mother had taught her to resist anyone trying to bully her.

Kadya stiffened. The woman walked over and

slapped her hard. Pain seared through her cheek. She thought she would lose her balance. But she caught herself and stood tall, staring solidly into the woman's hateful eyes.

She could not take anything more from her than she had already lost. She would never give this woman the satisfaction of seeing her suffer. She would do whatever was necessary to win this showdown.

The woman glared at her and cursed. She slapped her again. Kadya held her own, feeling she might faint. She braced herself as the woman reached for the stick used to tend the fire when Pita walked through the door.

The indescribable hopelessness she had seen in Pita's eyes made sense. Pita was terrified. She must have experienced brutality at the hands of this woman.

The woman looked at Pita, dropped the stick to the floor, and brushed past her. She left the hut in a wave of bitterness.

Pita came over to her and saw the redness of her cheeks. She rushed to grab a small square of rawhide. She dipped it in water and placed the moist cloth on Kadya's cheeks.

Tears sprang to Kadya's eyes for Pita's kindness. She took the cloth and sank onto the cot.

"Her name is Henna."

Pita sat beside her and said, "She will be back. She is taking you to the council. They will want to meet you. You were brought here for a reason. She is angry because she did not choose you."

Kadya was surprised to hear Pita speak so she could understand.

"I will never marry his son. I am not staying here. I will die before I marry anyone here," she said defiantly.

Pita sprang to her feet, eyes blazing in the firelight.

"Oh no, you must not say that. They will make you. They will hurt you!"

Kadya looked straight ahead, growing increasingly determined. "Let them," she said. "I have nothing left. They can take nothing from me."

Pita shook her head back and forth. The door opened. Henna returned with the young man from outside. Without a word, the young man took Kadya by the arm on one side. Henna grabbed her by the other. She almost fell as they pulled her forward to go with them. At least she was leaving behind this dreadful hut and would be outside where she could think of what to do next.

In the darkness, she could hear drums in the distance. When they reached the village, dancers cast shadowy silhouettes, parading around a fire to the sing-song rhythm. The crowd celebrated with hoots and shouts.

Kadya relaxed against the grip of her two escorts. She knew there was no use fighting them now. They loosened their hold on her arms, guiding her through the crowd. Kadya ignored the curious looks and stares. She thought it strange that this hateful woman now appeared proud as if she were responsible for Kadya's appearance at the evening's gathering.

When they reached the center of the village, Kadya was seated on a bearskin rug next to a beautiful woman with two small children. The woman wore long feathers from each earlobe. A child sat demurely in her lap with wide eyes like water droplets. She also held a baby wrapped tightly in a blanket, fast asleep.

On her other side was a man with a wrinkled face. His naked arms were skin and bones. His buckskin pants showed signs of neglect. He held his pipe in his mouth with dirty fingers. His smile revealed a missing tooth. Kadya shuddered at the smell of his breath.

The smoke from the fire led her eyes upward to the brilliant night sky. Kadya surveyed the assembled group. She felt she was in a dream. The dancers continued their display.

These people were unaware of her suffering. They had taken her family, destroyed her village, and had her kidnapped. But they could not see the stone she was hiding right in their midst.

The council entered the assembly wearing matching robes. They took their places on the other side of the fire. One of them wore layers of ornamentation around his neck. Kadya thought he must be the head of the council. The singing and drumbeats stopped. He stepped forward to speak. The crowd cheered. He waved for Durk and Raffi to step forward. The crowd roared with praise. Two ornately dressed children escorted them to their places of honor. He spoke in solemn tones to his excited audience. Kadya could not understand what he was saying. Tarek presented the stone from his waist pack. Proudly, he held it up as the crowd erupted with joy. Kadya watched the spectacle of the fake stone unfold.

Next, the children presented Tarek and Raffi with large necklaces made of feathers and beads. The drums began to play while dancers moved before the enthusiastic crowd.

The woman next to her shouted and clapped her hands. The children in her lap took it in stride.

Eventually, the music died down. Kadya assumed everyone would leave. But Henna returned and waited for her to stand. Kadya stood to her full height and returned her gaze. Henna turned away. This pleased Kadya after their earlier encounter. She squared her shoulders and took deep breaths while they paraded her before the council. She felt self-conscious and wanted to flee. Instead, she bowed in respect, as she would in her village, and waited for them to speak.

The council stared at her and gestured their approval. Two young children presented her with a delicate white beaded necklace. They waited for her to kneel and placed it around her neck. When she stood, the council showed their agreement with applause. The drums played again softly. Food was spread on large tables with several roasted boar for feasting.

Kadya looked across the flames at the people in their revelry. She wanted no part of this spectacle. She would find a way to escape. She had to.

As she scanned the crowd, across the fire she saw a beautiful woman staring at her with her forefinger pressed to her mouth in a gesture of silence. Their eyes locked.

Kadya gasped. It was her mother, Lania.

Kadya struggled not run to her. Instead, she stared, taking in the unbelievable sight of her mother, alive.

Next to her mother was a small child hanging onto her dress. The child was crying. She reached to comfort the child, and Kadya watched her mother pick up the child and walk away.

She turned to find Henna next to her. She walked her back to the small hut where Pita was waiting. Kadya said nothing. She collapsed on the cot and let the tears fall.

She was overwhelmed with emotion. Relief to see her mother alive, and desolation knowing she could not go to her. She wanted to tell her about Ruark and Tawnee and all they had endured.

Through her tears, she fell asleep. She dreamed of fire and smoke swirling about her mother's face. This time, her hands were outstretched. She held a glowing red stone.

Something jarred Kadya awake. She heard a faint sound outside the wall of the hut. It was only an animal, she assured herself, closing her eyes.

She pushed back the memory of the evening before, unable to forget the dream of her mother and the red stone. After a few moments, she heard the sound again. This time it was a tapping rhythm.

She gathered her courage and stood in the darkness. She hoped to find out what it was and set her mind at ease. Edging toward the opening of the hut, she almost stepped on Pita, sleeping right in front of it. Kadya froze. Pita made a noise and then rolled over. Kadya quickly stepped over her into the starlit night.

The night sounds and the cool open air greeted her. She tiptoed silently to the corner and peeked around the side of the hut where she had been sleeping. She could not see anything but shadows of hanging ivy.

Her heart stopped when she heard her name whispered. She could hardly believe it. She knew this voice. It had to be. In the darkness, she heard it again, only louder this time.

"Kadya, it is me. Over here."

Was she dreaming? She peered into the shadows. Slowly, she could see the outline of her mother.

Kadya fell into her arms without a sound. Tears streamed down her cheeks in silent sobs.

"Are you alright? Has anyone hurt you?" Lania whispered in alarm.

Kadya shook her head and mumbled weakly, "No."

"I saw you with Henna and I knew where to find you. This is where they brought me."

Lania held her at arm's length. "We must get away

from here tonight. Now is our only chance. It won't be easy. If we go back to our village, we can hide in our food cellar."

"I had the same idea," Kadya said quickly. "I kept track of landmarks and left behind stones to show the way. I had plans to run away if I could."

Lania held her close and whispered, "That's my girl. We are already on the edge of the village. We must make it up to the ridge."

"We must go now!" Kadya whispered, desperate to get away. She turned to run, taking Lania's hand. They moved fluidly, alert to any noise they might be followed.

When they were a safe distance away, they hid to catch their breath and ensure no one was behind them.

"I see you have the orange stone. I saw you had it right away."

"Yes, there is much to tell you. Will you take it now?" Kadya pulled it from the fold in her skirt relieved to give it to her mother. Lania quickly put it in her waist pocket.

"Can you keep going?" her mother whispered, unaware of all that Kadya had faced in the weeks since the attack. "We need to keep moving. We are likely being followed."

"Yes," Kadya answered confidently. She ripped the beaded necklace from her neck. Together, they climbed to the top of the ridge.

✳✳✳

Tarek watched the women escape from where he stood in the shadows. He followed their movements until they disappeared at the crest of the mountain. As he turned to go, he saw the white beaded necklace in the path before him, broken and scattered like stars across the sky, like the pieces of his heart.

84

Chapter 19

Tawnee awoke early. She wanted to see the pink stone. It was there, glittering in the darkness against the early morning sky. A few stars were visible, and she could see silvery clouds rising above the cliff. It would be morning soon. She thought about the other children. Were they still forced to walk every day with no comfort or care? Even if they were sick or injured? Tears filled her eyes to know they were suffering.

When she looked again at the pink stone, it grew brighter.

She hoped Ruark would find a way to get to the stone soon. She wanted to find Kadya. Tawnee worried she would never see her again. Closing her eyes, she decided to sleep longer. There was nothing she could do.

A few hours later, she woke up to sunshine. She was ready to go when Ruark returned from scouting the area. They headed out of the gorge into the valley to hike along the river. Tawnee was increasingly curious about the stones and full of questions.

"How can some people see the stones and others cannot?"

"The old ones say it is because some do not have pure hearts." He anticipated her next question before she asked it. "Being pure in heart means to have good intentions, to do what is right."

They walked down a steep slope to the river to find a place to cross.

"You said children always see them," Tawnee continued. "Some of the children could not see the orange stone the day I found it."

"They have to be shown." Ruark reached out his hand to help her. She jumped off a large rock to the sandy shore of the riverbed. "Then it is a choice. It is always a choice," he repeated.

In silence, they walked along the riverbank strewn with boulders and logs. They waited to find a place shallow enough for them to cross.

"When we get to the other side, we can fish for breakfast," he said. "Take my hand. The water is deep in the middle and moving fast. I will hold onto you."

Tawnee put her hand in his. They walked into the shallow side of the river. About halfway across, the channel dropped off. Tawnee slipped under the water but quickly found Ruark's arm. When they reached the other bank, Ruark lifted her onto one of the exposed boulders along the shore.

"That looks like a good fishing spot," he said. He motioned toward a quiet pool. "Gather some brush and sticks for the fire."

By the time she returned, Ruark threw a large trout out of the water near where she stood. She jumped away in excitement, watching it wriggle in the sand.

While Ruark got the fire going, Tawnee continued with her questions. "How are children shown what the stones mean?"

"They learn from those who came before them." The firelight reflected in his eyes.

"Like Mother and Father?" she asked from the fallen tree log where she was sitting. She watched Ruark stoke the fire and place the stick with the trout over it.

"Yes, like them, and now we must choose."

Tawnee looked across the river, hiding the tears filling her eyes again until Ruark called her to eat.

"We have quite a hike ahead of us. I found a place for us to stay."

"Can we bring Kadya when we find her?" Tawnee asked hopefully.

"Yes, we will bring Kadya to this place when we find her. Now go clean up while I pack up."

Tawnee knelt over the water to wash her hands and face. She trusted Ruark's words. She would see Kadya soon.

Chapter 20

Lania and Kadya traveled at night. They stayed hidden during the day. They were exhausted after walking for many nights.

"Tell me more about Ruark and Tawnee," Lania asked. They walked along the river. The moonlight overhead sparkled across the water.

Kadya knew her words comforted her mother. Thoughts of her children alive and well diminished the scars of loss and brutality. Kadya recounted everything Ruark did while she was with him and how he watched over them in the valley. They talked about the other children and how they were doing while she was with them. She talked about telling Tawnee the story of the wolf cubs and other happy stories to help her sleep. She told her about the stones.

"We found three of the stones. The blue stone of peace was in a cave and the yellow stone of abundance was behind a waterfall. They are beautiful together! The pink stone of empathy is high on a mountain, but we could not reach it. The stones were leading us, Mother."

"If the stones were leading you, they are still leading you, Kayda. They have been hidden all this time. We must prepare for what is to come," Lania said.

They stopped before dawn to sleep within the exposed roots of a tree. Lania took out the orange stone. The glow illuminated their faces and the branches of the tree that loomed above them.

"The stones of our ancestors are real," Lania smiled.

Chapter 21

Ruark and Tawnee followed a small stream up the mountainside. Pine trees clustered together, creating a dark canopy above them. Little vegetation grew in the dappled sunlight of the forest floor. The only sounds were the rippling water and the occasional muffle of their feet in the pine needles underfoot.

Ruark thought of Kadya. He hoped she had tried to escape using all she learned in the days they'd spent traveling. It would be his only chance of finding her.

"We have to be almost there," Tawnee said, interrupting his thoughts.

"We are," he answered. He directed her toward the stream.

"Wait here," he said. "I want to make sure no one is there."

Tawnee became alarmed, "Who?"

"I want to check it out before we go. Promise me you will wait here?"

"As long as I can see you."

Ruark edged around a boulder protruding into the path. The shelter was a distance away. But if he went closer, Tawnee would not be able to see him.

He watched for a few moments. A bow leaned against the wall near the opening of the shelter. A waterskin sat next to it on the ground. Ruark waited. He turned to see Tawnee watching him.

When he looked back, a man walked from behind the shelter. He limped and stopped to pick up the waterskin. Then he walked toward the stream.

Ruark's heart beat wildly. It was his father, Raul.

The realization his father was alive careened through his mind. He longed to run to him but could not move. The scene unfolded before him. Tawnee looked upstream at the man bending down at the water's edge. Her eyes were fixed, unable to trust what she saw. She turned to Ruark for silent permission to believe her eyes.

Slowly, she walked along the stream toward her father. He turned and recognized her. She ran to him and fell into his arms.

Ruark ran, too. Raul stood when he saw his son coming out of the darkness of the woods. He steadied himself and held out his arm while his son buried his face in his father's shoulder, shaking with emotion.

"Let me look at you," his father said.

Ruark stepped back so his father could see his face. "You are brave," he said with a smile. "And this one," he said, picking up Tawnee, "You have grown." He embraced them both again. "We have much to tell each other."

The three walked to the shelter. Raul held Tawnee's hand and leaned against Ruark for support.

Once inside, they sat and began to explain everything that had happened since that terrible day in the village.

Their father began, "I was coming back from a hunt

when I saw the smoke. It was the Malevo from the north. After three days, I was hit with an arrow. It was useless to follow them while I was injured so I headed back. I had to see if there was anything left of the village or if anyone was there. I wanted to search for you, but my leg was getting worse." He straightened it now. "I know they have your mother."

"I saw them take Mother away, and then they took me. I screamed, and he threw me over his shoulder," Tawnee said, reliving the memory.

"That was the worst thing of all. I knew the Malevo had taken you."

Ruark added, "They took her with the other children and forced them to search for the stones."

Raul stopped short and looked at her, then at Ruark. "They took the children to find the stones?"

"Yes, Father. They still have them."

"Do they have the stones?"

"They have the orange stone. I found it before Ruark found me," Tawnee asserted.

He looked at Ruark in alarm.

"How did you find it, Tawnee?"

"They made us search all day looking for the stones. They said I could see Mother again if I found one. But the men were lying. They only laughed when I asked to see her."

He gathered her in his arms. "You will see her again. You will see her again."

"Kadya and I found two of the stones in the first days after the attack. I felt the stones were leading us, Father. Then they captured Kadya, and now she is gone."

"Gone?" Raul dared not believe the rising fear in his heart.

"Yes. Two men took Kadya. She was sleeping near

me. In the morning they took her away," Tawnee said.

Ruark finished the story. "Kadya was with me on the day of the attack. We traveled together for many days until we found Tawnee. One night when Kadya and I were trying to rescue Tawnee, the men captured Kadya. That is how Kadya and Tawnee were together. I went back to rescue them, but Kadya was gone. I freed Tawnee and that is why we are here."

"How many days?" Raul's voice was tense.

"Today is the fifth day," Ruark answered.

"Tell me more about these two men who took your sister."

Tawnee told him all she could remember. How they laughed with Hatu and Durk and spent the night by the fire, and how they took Kadya away with them the next morning.

"I heard them take her. It woke me up."

"It was the Malevo. It had to be."

"Can we go find her?" Tawnee asked innocently. "Please, Father, can we go find her?"

"Yes," he said, determined to comfort his youngest daughter in the moment and rescue the other.

"Kadya is strong and brave," he continued. "She will know what to do."

"We found the pink stone," Ruark added.

"The pink stone? The stone of empathy? You have seen it?"

"Yes, we have seen it. I have the blue and yellow stones here." Ruark opened his pack and passed the stones to his father.

"I have never seen the stones' glow. I have only heard about them in the stories told to me by my father and grandfather. They are real?" Raul laughed gently. "Where is the pink stone?" he asked.

"It is high on the cliff. You can see it where the river bends." Ruark watched him adjust his leg, wincing at the pain.

"I went back to the village, Father. Have you been there?"

"No, I have not."

"There is nothing left. It was burned to the ground," Ruark said quietly.

"I had a feeling it was gone. We will rebuild. But first, we must find Kadya. Tomorrow we will head toward the Malevo camp. For now, we should rest and prepare something to eat."

***

Later, while Ruark and Tawnee slept, Raul stepped outside the shelter, vowing to keep his promise to Tawnee. He would not lose his wife and daughter to the Malevo. Since the attack, the days and nights had melted together. He had almost died from the pain and fever. The arrow had penetrated his leg, just below the back of his knee. But the pain of losing his wife and daughter was far worse.

He made a plan. It was a way to get to Kadya and Ruark would soon find out what he had in mind.

Chapter 22

Pak stared into the rushing water and threw another stone into the stream. He could not stop thinking about Ruark and his sisters. They were not like anyone he knew. The people in his village were selfish in comparison, always wanting more and never satisfied. Yet, Ruark and his sisters remained courageous despite their loss. It did not make sense.

Tawnee had found one of the stones. How was she able to see it? His people were obsessed with possessing the stones, but why? Chasing around the mountains to find stones seemed such nonsense to him now.

When he was young it made sense. The stories of the stones and their loss made him angry and filled him with vengeance. The anger fueled him, made him want to help in the search. Now, the stories made him sad. It was pointless. He hated watching the children in the group each day, missing their parents, and crying themselves to sleep.

Ruark and his sisters cared about each other. They were close, sharing secrets and laughing together. Pak's older siblings never showed him the same regard.

Now, Kadya was kidnapped and on her way to the Malevo village, to his village. This angered him. Secretly, he was glad Ruark had come for her. But he could never let his father know. The night his father sent him to follow Ruark and Kadya into the darkness, he was told to convince them to return and join the search for the stones. When he found them sleeping in a cave, he made the decision to let them go.

When he returned without them, he received a beating, but he did not care. No one should be forced away from their people. It was wrong to do what his people had done. Destroying their village and taking everything from their people was unacceptable.

Pak decided he could not go back to the camp. Having traveled downriver from the rest of the group, he found himself near a small tributary. The sound of the water to his left and the beautiful soaring pines above him filled him with peace.

His father might wonder where he was when he did not return, but it would be days before they would try to find him. He planned to be as far away as he could go. He knew how to take care of himself. It was better than staying with his father.

He stopped to fish and caught a brown trout by hand, like he saw Ruark do days ago. His sense of competition had come in handy. He had practiced until he developed the quick timing needed to catch his dinner. The satisfaction of cooking it over a fire gave him more confidence in his decision to leave. He would stay here for the night and decide his next move in the morning after he rested.

It was still dark when he awoke. He rubbed his eyes. On the other side of the stream was a red glow. He thought it strange and could not take his eyes from it.

He had never seen anything like it before. The light illuminated the side of a soaring rock wall, casting shadows of quaking aspen leaves and tree trunks. He stared into the red glow sleepily, unsure if he was dreaming.

He got up and found a narrow place to cross the stream. Cautiously, he walked toward the source of the strange red glow.

It was a stone. It had to be the red stone of legend. He stared in disbelief, pondering what it meant. Finally, he picked it up and held it. The red glow grew brighter, burning through the fear and hate he had always known.

For the first time, he knew what it felt like to not be afraid. He was free.

Chapter 23

There is nothing left," Lania said, kneeling in the rubble of her old home. She picked up a handful of ash and let it sift through her fingers.

Kadya watched her mother take in the devastation, her hopes vanishing, seeing everything she had worked for destroyed.

Lania's long hair blew in the wind. She stood and brushed the ashes from her dress. "Let us hope something is left of our food storage."

Kadya followed her mother up the familiar trail that led to a small, enclosed dugout protected by a stand of trees.

"Look, it is untouched!" Kadya exclaimed.

Once inside, they found stores of barley and may grass. Dried plums, wild cherries, and blackberries lined the walls beside piles of squash and pine nuts. Dried meat hung from ropes strung across the back of the small cavern. Several large pots sat on the floor by a few neatly stacked smaller pots and cups.

They would need to gather more food to survive the winter. But for now, they had a place to call home.

"We will rest here for a time. Then I want you to take

me to the valley where we might find Tawnee and Ruark."

Kadya agreed. She helped her mother clear an area to make a cooking fire. Lania placed several large stones in a ring. She set one of the larger pots on the stones to ensure it was level. Then, she arranged the kindling, twigs, and small sticks that Kadya gathered.

Thunderclouds were gathering overhead. Kadya stood closer to watch her mother start the fire.

"We will need more kindling," Kadya said. She turned to walk up the hillside and noticed a strange red glow flicker and fade away across the valley. She stared, waiting to see it again. She decided she must have imagined it and went back to gathering wood for the fire.

When she returned, she helped Lania prepare a delicious soup. For the first time in many days, they shared a warm and relaxing meal.

"Tomorrow, we will search for Ruark and Tawnee," Lania said, settling back to relax. She looked at the gathering clouds. "I wonder what Tawnee is doing now. What does she do when it rains? Is she sad? She is so young to go through this."

Kadya did not know what to say. She worried about Tawnee, too. It was best to keep distracted until they could go and search for her.

"Let me take your bowl. Can I get you something more to eat?" Kadya asked. She walked to the cooking pot to refill Lania's bowl and noticed the red glow again. It grew brighter and brighter. Someone was walking toward them. Finally, she recognized who it was.

Pak.

She walked into the clearing, ignoring her mother calling her back. She ran toward him. What did he want? Was Tawnee nearby?

When she reached him, she exclaimed, "Pak? What are you doing here?"

"I saw smoke rising across the valley. I wanted to know who it was," he said calmly. He looked past her to where her mother stood by the fire. "I hoped to find you."

"What do you want with us?" Kadya asked defensively. She did not want anyone to encroach on the little peace of mind and safety they had found.

"I mean no harm to you. I have news."

"You have the red stone," she interrupted.

"Yes, I have it."

"But how?" she began. Then she thought better of it. She remembered Ruark telling her to be wary of strangers. Was he able to see it?

"Please let me tell you all that I know," he pleaded.

Kadya was skeptical of finding Pak alone and wandering the hillside. She watched him closely.

"Please, let me talk to both of you," he urged. He looked past her at her mother.

He reached for the stone in his waist pack. He offered it to her. "As a sign of my trust, take it. I found it three nights ago when I left my father," he said, motioning toward the mountain.

Kadya stared at the pulsating glow but did not take it.

"Come," she said simply.

They walked up the hill to where Lania was waiting.

"This is Pak. He has news for us," she said. "This is Lania," she said to Pak.

"I have seen your son and daughter. They made their escape several days ago. I found them in a cave several nights from here. My father sent me to find them. I let them get away."

"Tawnee is with Ruark?" Lania gasped.

"Yes."

"How were they?" Kadya asked.

"They were well," he responded.

Lania sat back in relief, "What about the other children? Where are they?"

Pak shuffled uncomfortably before answering. "They are still with my father."

Lania's expression softened, "Your father?"

"Yes, he has the children. I left my father."

Kadya saw the sincerity in his eyes.

"I will find them and bring them here." He held out the red stone. "Please take it. Keep it as a sign that I will bring them back."

Kadya was doubtful. She dared not trust Pak. How could she believe he would bring them back?

Her mother took the stone gently in her hands without speaking. Tears of gratitude streamed down her cheeks.

"Find them, Pak. Please find them," she said.

Chapter 24

Ruark watched the valley from his view high on the hillside. His father and Tawnee were behind him on the trail traveling along the river. They moved much slower due to his father's injury and Tawnee's small frame.

They had devised a plan for finding Kadya and could lose no more time. Raul wanted to know as much as he could about the two men. He questioned Ruark and Tawnee about how they traveled, predictable campsites, and any familiar signs they left behind.

First, they had to find the Malevo camp. The sun was high in the sky. Ruark had been searching since dawn. He hoped to find the most recent fire rings. When he found the campsite, he would go back to meet Tawnee and his father. Their plan would come together once they knew the location of the Malevo party.

Cautiously, he went down the hillside, to walk along the river, looking for any possible evidence. Any moment, he might encounter Pak or one of the two men.

It was late afternoon when he spotted the extinguished fire rings. He examined them and blew on the embers. A tiny trail of smoke rose from the ash. He was very close.

He continued along the river until the smell of roasting meat froze him in his tracks. Quickly, he hid in the trees and continued to press through the undergrowth in the direction of the scent. Just beyond the edge of the trees around the bend in the river he saw them. The children were resting after a long day, waiting for something to eat. The men crouched around the fire, preparing the food.

Now that he knew their location, he needed to double back to find his father and Tawnee. Together, they would get as close as they could to enact their plan.

Chapter 25

Firelight flickered against the tiny forms lying around the fire. He heard a child wailing. Ruark watched the familiar routine through the trees. Eventually, the children grew still while the men reclined around the fire. When the fires grew dim and he was sure they were asleep, he ran to find Raul and Tawnee waiting in the trees a distance away from the Malevo camp.

"The larger man is on his back with his legs crossed. You take him. I'll take the other, lying on his side. He is facing away from the fire. The children are asleep."

He looked at Tawnee, "Are you ready?"

Tawnee nodded. She would wait for her cue.

Ruark and Raul crept across the meadow toward the sleeping forms of Hatu and Durk. Raul lunged across Durk's chest, grabbing his face and pressing it firmly into the ground. Ruark quickly tied Hatu's ankles together with the twisted cord of ivy he had braided together the night before.

Hatu was disoriented. Ruark turned him on his belly and tied his arms behind his back. Unable to move, he yelled in shock.

Durk groaned, unable to speak with his face smashed against the dirt.

Quickly, Ruark bound Durk's ankles. Raul swiftly turned his face to the other side, catching him off guard. Ruark grabbed his arms and tied his wrist securely with the remaining ivy cord.

The commotion woke the children. They sat up to watch the spectacle in the dim firelight. Tawnee rushed to reassure them. They gathered around her, confused.

The men writhed about.

Ruark's father nodded to him, "You go first."

Ruark grabbed Hatu by the feet and dragged him toward a stand of trees not far away, protesting the whole way.

Ruark left him lying on the ground to help Raul move Durk to another tree.

In turn, each man was stood up and twisted tightly to a tree with cords of ivy, unable to move.

Ruark and his father stood silent, noting their handiwork, waiting for them to stop and listen. The distant firelight illuminated their faces while they screamed vulgarities.

When they were finally quiet, Raul spoke firmly.

"Two men took my daughter. Where did they go?"

Hatu sneered and spat at the ground near his feet.

Raul turned to walk away. Ruark followed. Durk began to shout, begging them to come back, offering to tell them everything. Ruark and his father continued walking, showing no interest in what they had to say.

"Perhaps they will want to talk in the morning," Raul said with a hint of a smile to Ruark.

They walked to where Tawnee and the children were gathered. Raul spoke to each of them gently, to find out if they were hurt.

"You are safe now. We will stay here tonight and head in the direction of the village tomorrow. It will take a few days to get there. Now, I want you all to try to get some sleep."

It was difficult for them to settle down, so he sat next to Tawnee to calm them and wait for her to fall asleep. Ruark tended the fire and found a place to lie down.

After the children were settled, Raul looked out at the darkness. Somewhere out there, Kadya and Lania were living out their nightmares. The thought sickened him and made the pain in his heart hurt more than his leg.

He needed to rest. Hopefully, an answer would come. He stoked the fire before lying down to sleep. The sounds of nighttime calmed him.

When he woke, a hint of rose tinged the horizon. He wondered how Hatu and Durk were doing and trusted the ivy was strong enough to hold them. He hoped they were experiencing at least a taste of the suffering they had inflicted upon the children and the people of his village. He also expected to get the answers he needed from them to find Kadya.

Rising, he decided to go to Hatu and Durk and allow them to correct their responses from the night before. When he reached them, he saw Hatu standing against the tree with his head against the tree attempting to sleep. Durk was slumped over with his head completely down. In the light of day, he could observe Ruark's handwork. He had tied them up tightly. The hours they spent collecting, braiding, and knotting the ivy was worth it. He chuckled to himself.

Abruptly, one of them jerked awake, defiance returning as he noticed his captor watching.

"Where did they take Kadya?" Raul asked.

The man stared at him insolently. He had no intention of cooperating.

Raul shrugged and turned to walk away, determined to win this game. He would wait.

When he returned, Ruark was tending the fire.

"Did they tell you anything?" Ruark asked, not looking at him.

"No, but they had their chance."

Ruark shook his head in dismay.

"They can stay there as long as they choose," Raul said. He sat across from Ruark.

"If we can make it to the village, we have the storehouse. We can stay there."

Ruark agreed. "When do you want to leave?"

"When everyone is ready."

Chapter 26

The children ate their breakfast of dried meat and ground grain cakes. There was an air of excitement. They were no longer subject to the endless searching for stones.

Ruark had carried a heavy weight for many weeks. He was glad the children were safe, but he needed to tell his father what was on his mind.

"I want to get the pink stone," Ruark said. He looked back at the fire. He did not know why he felt so strongly.

"It will be dangerous," his father answered. Raul surveyed the horizon of snow-peaked mountains. "The stones cannot be possessed. You either receive what they offer or reject it."

Ruark knew his father was right, but it did not change his desire to secure the stone.

"Shall we give the men one more chance?" Raul asked. "Surely they are ready to talk now."

They walked across the meadow to find the men fully awake. They were still tied standing, tightly tied to a tree, and furious at their plight.

"We are leaving now. Tell me where my daughter is!"

They looked at each other in silence. Hatu scoffed,

"They took her back to our village. She is a young woman. It is time she married. It is perhaps a ten-day journey from here, that way," he said, nodding his head because he could not use his hands.

Raul walked closer to Hatu and took out a knife from his belt. He pressed it to the ivy binding on his chest. "And you will swear that what you have told us is true?"

Hatu screamed, fearing for his life. "Yes, yes! Everything I have said is true!"

Durk echoed, "It is true. Now let us go!"

Raul gave him a contemptuous look as he and Ruark turned to walk away.

Hatu and Durk yelled after them angrily.

"I did not say I would let you go," Raul said, over his shoulder.

Ruark and Raul continued walking, unmoved by their pleading.

When they got back to the camp, Ruark asked, "How shall we find Kadya?"

"I am not sure, yet. I must take the children back to the village. We will have the food shelter if it has not been destroyed. I want you to find the pink stone and bring it back to us. Then we will go find Kadya together."

It was midday when everyone was rested and ready to go. Ruark prepared to go in the opposite direction.

Raul hugged him tightly, "Take care, son. Return to us safely."

Tawnee ran to him and clung to him, "Be safe!"

He knelt and held her for a moment. He reached into his pack and took our Kadya's hairpin. He handed it to Tawnee. "Please keep this for Kadya. I will see you soon."

She took the hairpin and held it lovingly. She watched Ruark until he disappeared into the forest.

Chapter 27

Who did this to you?" Pak asked. He unwound the ivy and tore apart the knots that held his father to the tree.

"The boy and his father," Hatu yelled. He kicked impatiently at the vines tangled around his feet.

Pak said nothing while he untied Durk. Both men collapsed to the ground.

"Where have you been?" Hatu demanded.

"Thinking," Pak responded. He sat down in front of them. He handed them his water skin to offer them a drink.

"Why do our people search for the stones when we cannot see them? Why destroy the lives of others?"

Hatu scoffed at him.

Pak stood to go.

"I am leaving you and your ways," he said.

They must have spent days tied to those trees. They are blinded by hatred. He thought as he walked away. It made his decision easier.

"Wait, Pak!" his father called after him. "Where will you go? They took our supplies."

"Not all of them," he called back.

Pak kept walking. He had to keep his promise. He must find Ruark and Tawnee.

The sound of his father's yelling grew faint until, at last, he was out of earshot. He hoped his father would not follow him.

For three days, he traveled without any sign of Ruark or Tawnee. He had been so confident in his ability to track them. But now he was unsure.

He rounded the bend in the river beneath the shadowy birch and pine. He saw the pink light. It shone brightly, high on the cliffside across the valley.

Chapter 28

The wind grew stronger the higher Ruark climbed. He spent the entire day searching for a route to the stone. This side of the cliff was passable. It was steep, but there were passages he could follow. He made his way watching every foothold, trying not to look down.

The pink stone was within reach, but his father was right. It was dangerous. One misstep would send him careening into the valley. He moved with his back to the wall of the cliff, step by step, inching his way. He hung from an outcropping. His feet dangled beneath him before finding a secure foothold to continue.

Exhausted, he reached a narrow ledge lying flat on his belly. The wind was constant, adding to his fatigue. His hands were within inches of the pink stone embedded below. He had only to remove the stone and climb back to the safety of the shelter on the mountainside where he found his father.

His rest was interrupted. Someone was climbing toward him. The blood drained from his face. He peered over the ledge to see a familiar form struggling up the side of the cliff.

"Pak!" he shouted.

"I came to find you," Pak answered out of breath. He was too intent on finding his next hand or foothold to look up.

Ruark was not sure what Pak was talking about. Was it a trick? How could he know to find him in this place now when he was so close to the pink stone?

Pak climbed until he was eye-to-eye with Ruark. His body was pressed against the cliffside while his foot balanced precariously on a small ledge.

"Your sister is safe with your mother. They are staying near your village," Pak said, panting.

Ruark stared in disbelief. Could it be true?

Of course, Kadya would be at the food cellar if she was able to get there. That made sense, but their mother, too? He wanted to believe Pak's words.

"How did you find me?" Ruark asked.

Pak tried to answer, but his foot slipped off the rock.

He seized a small bush to catch himself to regain his footing.

Gravel and rocks plummeted down the cliff wall. He hung precariously from the sapling. The spines of the needles cut into his hands.

Ruark reached down to grab hold of him. Their eyes locked.

"Take my hand!" Ruark cried.

Pak fought desperately to hold on.

"Take my hand!" Ruark screamed again.

Pak's feet searched against the side of the cliff to find a hold.

Ruark watched helplessly. Pak hung in limbo, trying to find a place to secure his foot.

Pak reached for the pink stone and shook it loose from the wall of the cliff. Hanging there, he held it up to Ruark.

"Take it, take it!" he shouted.

The stone glistened between them brilliantly, pulsing its pink light.

"Take my hand!" Ruark yelled again, desperate to save Pak from falling.

Pak refused and held the stone out to Ruark. His eyes pleading.

Ruark took it and reached for Pak's hand, trying to secure him, but he was not fast enough. Pak's hand slipped off the sapling at the same time.

Ruark was afraid to look down, afraid to move. Tears burned in his eyes. He looked at the glistening stone in his hand in horror. The stone faded until it no longer gave its soft pink light.

He allowed despair to engulf him. Sorrow and pent-up grief wracked his body. He cried until he fell asleep. The afternoon sun slipped away.

Chapter 29

Ruark will stay inside the trees during the day and come down to the river in the evening. He will want to make sure Tawnee is safe. They will make camp up the hill," Kadya said confidently. She knew how Ruark traveled.

"We should leave first thing tomorrow," Lania said. "We can walk for a day and wait. Then we can go another day if we must. I hope they are close. I do not want to get too far from our food storage."

Kadya could hear the concern in her mother's voice.

"We will find them, Mother."

Lania rolled their supplies into a large piece of rawhide and tied it with vines. Kadya handed her the net she had made of vines. They would use it to catch fish. Lania secured the net to the pack.

Kadya finished wrapping the dried food they would need for two days of travel. She stood and looked toward the river. The afternoon sun was warm. They would need to prepare their evening meal.

For a moment she could not believe her eyes. A small girl was running up the hill side.

Tawnee?

"Mother, look!"

Lania saw Tawnee. She dropped what she was doing and ran the distance to meet her. Kadya followed.

Tawnee flung herself into her mother's arms.

"Tawnee! You are safe!" Lania cried.

Tawnee was breathless and did not speak.

"Where is Ruark?" she asked.

Tawnee pulled back, not letting go of her mother. "He went to get the pink stone. I came with Father and the children. They are coming. Father let me run ahead when we saw you were here."

Lania looked at Kadya.

"So, Father and the children are coming?" Kadya asked.

"Yes, there they are," Tawnee pointed.

"Father was hurt. He walks very slowly."

"How was he hurt?" Lania asked.

"It is his leg."

Lania put Tawnee down. She looked toward the river's edge.

Kadya embraced her sister and watched her mother shield her eyes from the sun's glare.

There, walking along the river, was her father and the band of children with him.

Kadya took Tawnee's hand and they followed Lania toward the river.

When she reached Raul, they both knelt to the ground. They held each other in a long embrace. The children ran ahead.

Kadya watched the reunion of her mother and father. She watched her mother ask questions and saw her father patiently reply. Slowly her mother helped him stand.

When he reached Kadya he held her tightly.

"Ruark told me the Malevo took you. I hope they did

not harm you."

"No, Father. It was difficult but they did not hurt me. Mother was there. We escaped together and came here."

The weary group made their way to the cooking fire outside the food dugout.

Before her father sat down, Kadya asked, "Where is Ruark?"

"He went to get the pink stone. He told me how the two of you found the other stones," he laughed gently.

"He did not think we could reach the pink stone," Kadya said, concerned.

He took Kadya's arm for support and sat down. He was eager to rest his leg.

"Mother and I have the orange and red stones too," she added.

"How? You must tell me."

"There will be time. The children are hungry. I must help prepare the food."

"Kadya, your brother will return," Raul said reassuringly. "I believe he will find much more than the pink stone."

"I hope he returns soon," she answered.

She turned to find Tawnee standing in front of her, hand outstretched, holding the hair rod Kadya thought was lost forever.

"I saved it for you."

Kadya took it and sank to the ground. She hugged her sister.

"Thank you, Tawnee."

Chapter 30

Ruark woke in the night to the howl of a wolf. Pak's face flashed before him. Pak had given everything to help him. Finding him now was the least he could do.

Grief consumed him. He rested his head against a rock. The howling stopped.

At dawn, he dared to look down. He could not see where Pak fell. He began his trek into the valley. He feared the worst. He traced the cliff wall. Still, he saw no sign of him.

By afternoon, Ruark decided to climb the steep rise. He climbed in the direction he believed Pak would be and soon found him lying on a narrow ledge. He decided to spend the night on the side of the mountain with Pak's lifeless body. It was the only honorable thing to do. Leaving Pak alone was not an option.

When he reached Pak, he was still. His eyes were closed. He could see abrasions on the side of his face. He found a place to sit near Pak.

Ruark was exhausted. Familiar tears filled his eyes again. How had it come to this? He was afraid to look at the stones in his pouch. There were three of them now, but they no longer offered their light. He knew exactly when his sight changed.

Now, his tears seemed useless, but they just kept coming. If only he could go back and leave the pink stone where it was, none of this would have happened.

He lay in the deafening silence. Darkness descended across the cliff. Countless stars twinkled above the desolate landscape. The chill of the night settled around him. Ruark fell into an uneasy sleep.

He was startled awake by a sound he could not identify. He waited to hear it again, but there was nothing. As he settled back to sleep, he was urged awake again by the sound of groaning. He sat up in the darkness. The noise was unmistakable.

"Pak!" he whispered.

Pak moaned weakly but did not move.

"Pak? Ruark whispered again, "It's me, it's Ruark! You are alive. You fell. Do you remember? I am going to get you down from here! In the morning, we will figure out a way."

Pak was silent.

Ruark waited for the pink sunrise and any sound from Pak. He closed his eyes to rest a little longer until daylight. He would need strength for the task ahead.

He had no idea how he would get Pak off the side of the cliff. He hoped the morning would bring the answer.

When there was enough daylight, Ruark dared to look up to the place above him where the pink stone was located the day before. Pak must have slid down to where he was now instead of falling the whole way.

Ruark looked at Pak and the narrow pathway. He would have to drag him down. It was not going to be easy, and it was going to be dangerous. Pak had made no sound since the middle of the night.

He surveyed the horizon and saw the wolf again. It was on the forested side of the mountain looking back at him. Was it there to guide him? Maybe he should not try to go down the cliff but work his way toward the forest. There might be less risk of falling.

"Pak?"

He did not respond.

"Pak? Wake up."

Pak moved his eyelashes, struggling to open his eyes.

"It is Ruark. You fell. You are hurt. I want to move you off this cliff."

Pak managed to open his eyes at last. He recognized Ruark and moaned in pain.

"Where does it hurt?" Ruark asked.

He did not move but attempted to speak. He made a sound in his throat.

Ruark moved closer to hear Pak say more, but he closed his eyes and passed out.

Pak was not ready to be moved. Ruark was unwilling to risk it until he knew more about his injuries. He would have to wait.

Ruark sat there in the stillness of the early morning, wondering what to do. He thought about his family and pictured each of their faces. They had survived the attack. It was only a matter of time before Ruark would see them. First, he had to get himself and Pak off the mountain alive.

He worked his way to the edge of the cliff. While Pak gathered strength, he could mark a path and get food and water. Carefully, he began the arduous climb, scrambling over rocks and narrow stretches of gravel until he reached the forest's edge. It would take twice as long to get Pak the same distance.

Ruark hiked further down the stream from the shelter where he and Tawnee had found their father. He drank and filled his water skin. Pak would need water to survive.

He could not eat enough of the berries he found growing along the stream. He wanted to hunt for something savory, but he had left his bow at the shelter. He emptied his wait pack of the stones and stuffed it with berries. It would be better to leave the stones here than to risk losing them on the mountain. Besides, he could no longer see them glow.

But what if they were lost? He marked the area where he placed the stones and left them under a small bush. He did not notice their faint glow in the shadows.

He planned to move Pak off the mountain by nightfall. Feeling refreshed, he retrieved his bow from the shelter and set off for the mountain. The sun was high in the sky. It was late morning.

Pak had not moved, but his eyes were open. He was staring at the sky. He moved his eyes toward Ruark without expression.

Ruark knelt beside him and gave him a small sip of water. Pak drank slowly. Ruark gave him another drink and sat down.

"I want to move you from this mountain. You have had a terrible fall. Do you remember it?"

Pak moved his eyes toward Ruark in faint recognition. He did not respond.

Ruark continued, "We were near the pink stone. You reached the pink stone and fell when you handed it to me." Ruark's voice broke.

Pak became agitated and made a raspy sound from his throat again, "No," he said. After a few moments he mustered his strength. "Can't move."

Ruark did not want to believe it. The fall that should have killed him left him unable to move.

"I think I can get us down from here."

"Let…me…be," Pak said slowly, forcing the words.

"No!" Ruark said, a bit more emphatic than he should have. He could not leave Pak to die on this mountain alone. Ruark leaned back. He had to think. Was if something worse happened to Pak while moving him? Did he have a choice?

Ruark decided instantly. "Where does it hurt?"

He searched Pak's eyes for the answer but found nothing. Pak had gone back to staring at the sky. Ruark offered him another drink, which he refused.

Determined, Ruark dragged Pak gently and picked him up by the shoulders. He pulled him onto his back to begin the difficult trip across the boulders and sandy patches he had marked earlier in the day. When Ruark needed to climb, he laid Pak on the boulder and carefully dragged him until he could carry him again. He stopped to rest many times.

Pak was unresponsive. At times, Ruark was unsure if he was dead or alive. He only knew that he needed to get him off the mountain.

By late afternoon, Ruark reached the edge of the forest. The shade now protected them from the heat of the sun. He laid Pak on his back. His eyes were still closed.

He would hunt or fish for dinner and return to set up camp. He had moved Pak far enough for now.

The shelter was upstream. He retrieved his bow and returned to Pak to wait for any game to wander by. He tended the fire and watched for any movement from Pak. The smell of cooking meat might encourage him to eat.

"Water," Pak said suddenly, "Water."

Ruark rushed to Pak's side and offered him sips of

water. He took some berries and squeezed the sweet juice into Pak's mouth, which he accepted.

When Pak closed his eyes, Ruark tended the fire and fell asleep.

Pak's restlessness woke Ruark. He offered Pak more water and berries.

Early the next day, he retrieved the stones from their hiding place and got more water. The stones did not offer their light.

He gathered sticks and vines to make a *travois* for carrying Pak. He tied large poles together and made a bed. He hoped he was strong enough to pull Pak back to the village. It would be slow going and take several days, but it was his only hope. He stopped his work frequently, to offer Pak sips of water and berry juice. Pak said nothing and stared straight ahead.

By evening, he completed his work with the *travois*. He hoped they could leave first thing in the morning and make good time on their journey home to his village.

Ruark placed a berry in Pak's hand to see if he could feed himself. His hand was limp. Gently, he helped Pak grasp the berry. He bent his arm at the elbow and raised his hand to his mouth to remind Pak how to eat.

Pak took the berry into his mouth. Ruark offered him meat from his stash. He was encouraged to know that Pak was developing an appetite and able to eat.

Pulling the *travois* was difficult. Ruark had to stop several times to reposition Pak when he slid off the bed with the movement. He tied Pak tightly to the bed to secure him.

By midday, he stopped to rest and give Pak a drink.

"Leave me here," Pak said feebly.

Without answering, Ruark wrapped his hand around the waterskin, putting it to Pak's lips so he could drink.

Pak willingly took the drink but refused to look at Ruark.

"I will not," he said at last. "I am taking you with me."

Ruark took Pak's other hand and moved it back and forth at the elbow. Then he took each of his legs and bent them at the knees.

Pak stared blankly at the sky.

The rest of the day, Ruark continued the slow way toward home. The *travois* bumped and tipped with each step. He struggled to pull it through narrow passes and low-hanging branches along the river.

By evening, he found a place to camp for the night and built a fire. Exhausted, he went to the river to fish. After feeding Pak, he gazed at the stars until he fell asleep.

Chapter 31

Little rain fell since the attack. The berries and edible plants that remained were withered and hard to find. Every bit of food was necessary for the upcoming winter.

Since her father's return with the children, she kept busy preparing food for everyone. She taught the older children to catch fish with the nets she made of vines.

Her parents planned how they would build the lodging they needed for everyone. She would go hunting with her father since Ruark had not returned. They needed to hunt large game to have the necessary supplies. They hoped others would find their way back to the village as they had. They would not give up hope that others had survived.

***

Kadya pulled on a stubborn weed and accidentally unearthed a wild beet. It was not ready. She was about to give up when she saw an unusual flash of light near the river. Someone was coming. She watched the light get closer. It changed from yellow to blue and pink. It was the glow of the stones. It had to be Ruark!

He was pulling something behind him. She ran to him.

Ruark gently put the poles down when he saw her and walked to meet her.

She clung to him. "I thought I would never see you again," she cried.

Ruark did not answer.

Kadya noticed Pak, lying on the *travois*. She ran to him. "What happened?"

"He is not able to move. He fell."

"Not able to move?" she repeated, kneeling to see for herself.

Pak turned his head slightly.

Kadya looked at Ruark. He gave a pained look.

"I am to blame. It happened on the mountain," Ruark said.

Kadya did not understand his confession.

"Take him to Mother," she said urgently.

Ruark took the poles and put them over his shoulders. He pulled Pak forward as Kadya followed behind, now aware of Pak's suffering and her brother's pain.

Amidst joyous cries, the seriousness of Pak's injuries was clear to see. Raul walked to meet Ruark and helped him drag the *travois* up the hillside.

"I cannot believe Pak survived the journey, let alone the fall," Raul said. He helped to lift him onto a bed of furs. They made him comfortable so he could rest.

Ruark told them what he had been doing for Pak.

Everyone agreed it should continue.

"Ruark saved my life. He could have left me behind, but he refused." Pak's voice trailed off.

Lania knelt beside him. "You gave up everything to bring our family together," she said. "You are part of our family now."

A brief smile crossed his lips for the first time.

Ruark took the stones out of his pack. The colors pulsed gently in soft hues.

Kadya did not know he had lost his ability to see them.

He laid them on the ground.

She heard him whisper, "I can see them. I can see them."

She did not understand why his eyes filled with tears.

"Peace, abundance, and empathy," Kadya said quietly. "Words to live by."

Lania placed the orange and red stones with the others. "Let us not forget healing and courage."

Kadya marveled at the message of her ancestors.

Chapter 32

After the evening meal, the family sat around the fire. Tawnee sat next to Ruark. Kadya sat with the children. Pak lay on the bed of furs beside Lania and Raul.

Ruark watched his father as he stood and began to speak. He held each of the stones up, one by one.

"The blue stone of peace was found first. It was high on a cave wall. When we choose peace, it spreads to others." He placed it on a small platform he had made of logs and covered in skins.

"The orange stone offers healing from disease and loss. Tawnee, Kadya, Lania?" he said slowly, "the orange stone protected you while you were gone. It brought you back to us."

He set it down and picked up the red stone. He looked at Pak. "You made a difficult decision, and the stone of courage was there when you needed it most." He placed it with the others.

He lifted the yellow stone. "Abundance. This stone reminds us to see the good in everything and everyone. To live with a sense of abundance, not lack." He placed it beside the others.

Solemnly, he took the pink stone in his hand. "The pink stone of empathy was the most difficult to reach. Ruark and Pak found it high on the mountain." He looked at Ruark. "Empathy is the most difficult of all to achieve." He placed it with the other stones. "It is possible this is the reason the stones were lost long ago. We must never forget this."

"Two of the stones are missing. The stone of wisdom and the stone of harmony. Perhaps they will lead us to find them when we are ready."

He picked up the stones and passed them around. The colors reflected from their faces as they held each one in turn. When everyone was finished, he took them back and placed them together by the fire.

"Accept their offerings. Experience their power. Let it guide your life."

He took his place next to Lania.

Together, they watched the light of the stones shine brilliantly against the starlit sky.

Ruark looked around at the familiar faces he loved, grateful to be home, and grateful to see again the stones' shimmering lights.

Author's Note

It has been such a pleasure to put these words onto the pages of my book. I began writing *The Seven Stones* for my third-grade class, one chapter a week. But by the time school ended, the story was not told. Later when I returned to finish it, I found the characters had grown and their world was examining and formulating ideas about life. It occurred to me that bringing focus to the many attributes that make life good for all and exposing the autonomy and responsibility we have in making choices regarding those attributes might give direction to troubled times. Choosing the stones to represent these attributes was pure joy and shall remain my secret for now. But discovering these characters as I wrote made me dig deep to find the essence in all of us that unites us and makes us human. Ruark and Kadya are much like you and me, with the same grit and determination we develop as we grow and mature. It is my hope, dear reader, that like me, you find yourself in these characters as you reflect on creating and leaving the world a better place for everyone.

About The Author

Kimberly Ashley is a writer and educator with a master's degree in Curriculum and Instruction and over twenty years of class-room teaching experience. She enjoys writing stories for her students that engage them in literacy and a love for reading.

As a child, farm life and peering into the dark skies of the Kansas prairie fueled her imagination and sparked her desire to understand how everything connects to the present. A reader of biographies and non-fiction, she weaves new understanding into the characters of her stories, to entertain and enlighten her readers about the plight of the human experience.

Besides teaching, her passions include music, anthropology, neuroscience, and philosophy. She loves hiking in the mountains, walking on the beach, and creating restful, creative spaces. She is a mother of four, grandmother of two, and lives in Lawrence with her cat, Dawkins.

Other Books to Enjoy From Anamcara Press LLC

ISBN: 9781941237-33-5
$18.99

ISBN: 9781941237-30-4
$18.99

ISBN: 9781941237-32-8
$18.95

ISBN: 9781941237-13-7
$18.95

ISBN: 9781941237-18-2
$14.95

ISBN: 9781941237-08-3
$24.95

Available wherever books are sold and at:
anamcara-press.com

Thank you for being a reader! Anamcara Press publishes select works and brings writers & artists together in collaborations in order to serve community and the planet.
Your comments are always welcome!

Anamcara Press
anamcara-press.com